FANGS

The Baron Blasko Mysteries
Book 1

A. E. Howe

Books in the Baron Blasko Mysteries Series:

FANGS (Book 1)

KNIVES (Book 2)

Copyright © 2018 A. E Howe

All rights reserved.

ISBN: 0-9997968-4-4
ISBN-13: 978-0-9997968-4-9

This book is a work of fiction. Names, characters, places and incidents are the product of the author's imagination or are used fictitiously. Any resemblance to actual events, locales, business establishments, persons or animals, living or dead, is entirely coincidental.

Except as permitted under the U.S. Copyright Act of 1976, no part of this publication may be reproduced, stored in a retrieval system or transmitted in any form or by any means, electronic or mechanical, including photocopying, recording or otherwise, without written permission from the author. Thank you for respecting the hard work of this author.

PROLOGUE

"I told you, Miss Josephine! I told you!" Grace Dunn shouted as she barged her way through the back door.

The solidly built, middle-aged woman was breathing hard as she came charging into the hallway, still yelling. "That monster has killed him, as sure as I'm breathin'! You got to do something, Miss Josephine. He's Satan's puppet." She rounded the bannister and started up the stairs. "I don't care what Mr. Roosevelt says, fear ain't the only thing we got to fear. We got to be afraid of that killer you got living in the basement."

Josephine Nicolson came out of her bedroom, where she'd been dressing for dinner, pulling her robe tight around her shoulders. "What are you screaming about?" she said, watching Grace pound up the stairs toward her.

"I have warned you and warned you! What'd I say?" Grace yelled now, huffing as she mounted the last steps to the second floor.

"Please keep your voice down," Josephine said, "and tell me what you're talking about."

Grace took a moment to catch her breath now that she'd conquered the stairs. Her dark skin was slick with sweat as she visibly pulled herself together.

"Mr. Erickson, dead in his bed. Found just now by Myra. Killed. Murdered! And we all know who did it." Grace's chin was up and her jaw clenched.

The two women were now standing face to face at the top of the stairs. Grace was short and full bodied while Josephine was taller and a few years younger, but both of them had stubborn eyes that were locked on each other.

"We don't know anything. You say Mr. Erickson is dead. Who told you this?"

"I heard it directly from Myra. She saw him lyin' there in his own blood," Grace answered, her voice laced with a certain flair for the dramatic.

Josephine wasn't surprised that Grace had heard it directly from Myra. The two maids were close friends who often spent their days off together. However, Josephine also knew Myra's tendency to exaggerate. She turned away from Grace and walked to the window that looked out from the second floor hallway onto the front lawn and across the street to the Ericksons' house. Sure enough, the last light of the day revealed a number of cars, horses and wagons parked or tied up across the street in front their house.

Josephine walked back to where Grace was standing, wearing an *I told you so* smirk on her face. "Until I know more, you're to keep quiet about our guest in the basement," Josephine told her, watching the smirk evolve into a deep frown.

"You got to get him out of the house, Miss Josephine. He's going to murder us in our beds," Grace insisted, her eyes locked on Josephine's.

The two women stood inches away from each other with feet planted, Grace's hands on her hips and Josephine's arms crossed in front of her. They both held strong opinions about their current houseguest, but Josephine wasn't so sure that Grace was wrong.

CHAPTER ONE

Six months earlier...

"I'm sorry, Miss Nicolson, but I can't do anything more for your father other than make him comfortable. His body is failing him," Dr. McGuire said, packing up his black bag.

Josephine thanked the doctor and walked him out the front door. The large Victorian house already felt as though it were in mourning. Nothing Josephine or Grace did seemed able to bring in more light or fresh air.

With a sigh, Josephine entered her father's room. Originally the front parlor, the space had been turned into a makeshift hospital room for Andre Nicolson. The man looked old and frail beyond his sixty-seven years, lying underneath the feather comforter on his large four-poster bed. It had taken five men and a master woodworker to disassemble it and carry it downstairs four months earlier.

"Josie, come here," he called to her. His eyes brightened just a little at the sight of his daughter, her honey-brown hair illuminated by the afternoon light coming in through the lace curtains.

"Papa." She sat down beside the bed and clasped his hand in both of hers.

"Ol' Doc McGuire told me the truth for a change. Of

course, he didn't need to. I know I'm not going to get better."

"Don't listen to him. That old fool doesn't know anything."

"Ha, you are the worst liar I've ever met. I should have taught you better."

"We shouldn't have let them operate on you," Josephine said regretfully.

"Hush that kind of talk. We did what we thought was best. Who knows. I might already be lookin' up at six feet of dirt if it wasn't for the surgeons. And they never promised nothin'." His breath became raspy. Josephine picked up the glass of water beside the bed and put it up to his mouth. He took a small sip, knowing better than to argue with her.

Their black cat, Poe, chose that moment to jump up on the bed, curling into a ball on Andre's chest. He stroked the animal, his mind in turmoil as he tried to decide if he should burden Josephine with his guilt. Keep it to yourself, Andre, his conscience told him. Take it to the grave with you. But another voice, one fueled by regret, told him to talk, to unburden himself to his daughter. He wanted to settle his accounts as best he could. Deep down, he feared the grave and the unknown beyond the veil. Though he'd been born in this country, his parents were from Romania and his childhood had been swaddled in the superstitions of the old country.

"Josie," he said softly.

"Yes, Papa?" she said, leaning down to hear him.

"I have something to tell you." He stopped, still struggling with his decision.

"What is it?"

"Your grandfather... My father was an odd man."

"I remember that," Josephine said, smiling at the memory of the curmudgeon who'd shaken his finger at her, telling her that tomboys would always meet a bad end. But then he would show her how to make her own wooden sword so they could have mock pirate battles around the front porch.

She had always enjoyed the time she spent with her grandfather, Grigore, but even as a child she had been aware of a darker side to him. It was a part of himself that he reserved for dark nights when he and the other men would retire to another room for bourbon and cigars. And there was no doubt he could be a hard man. She'd heard him berate her father for imagined indiscretions more than once.

"When he was dying, he asked me to do something for him. Made me promise." Her father's eyes seemed to be focused on that spot in time ten years earlier when he had sat beside his father's deathbed as Josephine now sat beside his.

"What?" Josephine prompted.

"There." Her father pointed to a vase on the large marble mantel above the fireplace. "In that vase are some of your grandfather's ashes. He asked me... Made me swear I would take his ashes back to the old country and scatter them in the graveyard of his village in the Carpathian Mountains." He paused, breathing heavily as he tried to catch his breath. "I thought I had more time. No, no, that's a lie. I thought it was a foolish request from a querulous old man."

Josephine could see the tears welling up in his eyes. "You and your father didn't always see eye to eye. I know that."

"True. We were different. He was always the stern man of business. He never forgave a debt. Never."

"And you feel like you owe him something now?"

"I do." He grasped her hand tightly. "I should have done what I promised. Now... I don't want to think that I..."

"I'll do it," Josephine said without hesitation. She would have promised anything to make him better.

Andre squeezed her hand harder, pulling himself up from the bed a few inches. "Don't say you'll take it to the old country unless you mean it." He was looking her square in the eye as though trying to read her thoughts.

"I swear. I will take Grandfather's ashes to Romania."

Andre sighed. "What have I done? Forgive me for burdening you with this task."

"Papa, I'll do it. I've always wanted to see a bit of the

world." Josephine wiped the tears from her eyes. "Don't think about it anymore. Just rest. I promise you, it'll be done."

He lay back in the bed and closed his eyes. Josephine gently removed her hand from his and stood up, looking more carefully at the vase on the mantel. It was a large blue vase that dated back to the last century. She hadn't even realized her grandfather's ashes were in the house, though she vividly remembered the local furor the day her father took the body to Montgomery. The fact that her grandfather was being cremated had been big news in the small town of Sumter, Alabama. Most folks had never heard of such a thing. But ten years ago, before the stock market crash and the onset of the Great Depression, every day had seemed to bring about new and different ways for people to spend their money.

Looking at the vase, Josephine wondered what she'd gotten herself into by promising her father she'd carry the ashes all the way to Romania.

The next morning, Andre Nicolson passed away. Jerry Connelly and some men from Connelly's Funeral Home came and took the body away so that it could be prepared for the viewing.

"Don't you worry, Miss Josephine, I'll look after him like he was my own," the mortician told her as they placed the body into the hearse.

"We're going to have the viewing on Friday," Josephine told him.

The funeral would be huge. Andre Nicolson had owned the only bank left in town after almost four years of the Great Depression. New York and Chicago had been hit hard and early, but in southern Alabama the effects had grown over time. Eventually, two of the town's banks had collapsed, leaving only Nicolson's Bank of Sumter still open and solvent.

"We'll have him back by tomorrow afternoon. Your father made all the preparations a couple of months ago. There's nothing for you to trouble yourself over," Connelly said with just a hint of Ireland in his accent. He'd been born in Semmes County, but his father and mother had immigrated just before the War Between the States. His father had carried a piece of Yankee steel in his leg until the day he died and, when Jerry had prepared his father for burial, he'd removed that reminder of the cruel war with the words, "Aye, there, that won't be bothering you anymore." Connelly had put the piece of shrapnel inside the same box that held his father's old Colt Army revolver.

After Connelly left, Josephine walked through the house, feeling like a stranger.

"You knew this day was goin' to come," Grace told her.

Grace had worked with Anna, the cook, and Jerome, the yard man, to get the house in proper order for the viewing and the gathering after the funeral. Even though neighbors and friends had brought enough food to feed a small army, under Anna's scrutiny much of it had gone to the farms to feed the dogs. Anna inspected every dish that came in the door, declaring only a few good enough to be laid out for the mourners.

"He went downhill so fast," Josephine said.

"The cancer will do that. I've seen 'em working one day and in the grave the next month. The good Lord does what he knows is best. Now you just rest. We'll have everything ready for the visitors," Grace said, easing Josephine over to the sofa.

The maid couldn't imagine not having any family. Her extended clan stretched out far and wide into all corners of Semmes County. When they got together for a marriage or a funeral, there wasn't room for anyone else. But here was Josephine, with her mother laid in the grave years ago of the fever and her father now ready to be placed in the churchyard beside her. Other than a few aunts and cousins scattered across the country, Josephine had no one. Grace just shook her head.

The viewing and the funeral went smoothly, with most of the town showing up to pay their respects to a man whose careful handling of the bank's and his customers' finances had left the community with more than most in these hard times of the boll weevil and economic uncertainty.

On Monday, Josephine tapped on the door of the bank well before opening time. She was let in by Martin, the head clerk. Her father had insisted that neither he nor Josephine should have a key to the bank. Due to Prohibition and the Depression, banks had become the prime targets of a new style of gangster. There had been quite a few bank owners who had been accosted at night and forced to open their banks by desperate men.

Andre Nicolson had thought that, if it was widely known he and Josephine didn't actually have a key to the bank or the safe, then they would be in less danger. One key was held by the bank manager and another by the county sheriff, in the event of an emergency. The bank manager also held a key to the safe, as did the head clerk. In a world populated by Baby Face Nelson, Pretty Boy Floyd and a host of others, Andre Nicolson had refused to take chances. Still, Josephine chafed at the thought of not having her own key to the bank.

She wished Martin a good morning and went straight back to Daniel Robertson's office and knocked on the door. The bank manager greeted her with a lowered head. He wore a black armband in mourning for her father.

"I wasn't expecting to see you for a while," Robertson said kindly. He was a small, older man who still wore Edwardian attire and a full beard. His hands constantly fidgeted whenever he wasn't working on account sheets.

"I need to discuss some business with you," Josephine said, looking around the office where she had spent so many hours. After her mother had died, her father had gotten into the habit of bringing Josephine to the bank when he was working.

"Of course. I'm at your service," Robertson said sincerely. He'd worked for the bank almost from the day it was founded in 1911 and felt a strong attachment to both Josephine and her father.

"First, I'd like to have a key to the bank," she said, watching as Robertson leaned back in his chair and took another look at her.

"Miss Josephine, you know why your father didn't keep a key. I think it would be very unwise…"

"I can take care of myself." She opened her purse and showed him the Colt revolver she kept with her. "I assure you."

Robertson blanched, even though he knew she could handle a gun. She'd gone dove hunting ever since she was a child, but he still wasn't comfortable with the thought that she could be forced to face down a hardened criminal. These days, even he felt nervous as he opened the bank in the morning. He would let his eyes roam suspiciously over anyone standing within a hundred feet of the bank whenever he put his key in the door.

"I know you can handle a firearm. That's not the point," he protested.

"I insist."

Her ego wasn't the only thing at issue. Josephine knew how easy it would be for the men who ran the bank on a daily basis to take her for granted. If she showed any weakness at the start, she would be at risk of losing control of the business. She'd thought long and hard about her new role since she'd learned she'd inherit the bank in a matter of months instead of years. Her choice was to sell her shares or to exercise control. She'd decided, at least in the short run, to keep control of the bank. Eventually she'd have to decide if she wanted to continue to chair the bank's board of directors, but that decision could wait.

"Of course. We have another key in the vault. I'll get it for you."

Robertson stood up stiffly and walked out of the office, his posture telegraphing his unhappiness with the situation. That's fine, Josephine thought. She wanted everyone to know that she was not going to conform to anyone's ideas about how she should act.

When Robertson came back, he laid the key on his desk in front of her with a scowl. "Is there anything else I can do for you?"

Josephine held up the key. "I don't want you to think that this is because I don't trust you. Father had a great deal of faith in you and I do too."

"I appreciate that. I would never let you or the bank down."

"I will be going out of town for at least three weeks, and possibly a month or more." She set the key back down on the desk. "I'd like you to put this key in the safe until I return."

Robertson's mouth opened and closed several times, and the areas of his face not covered by his beard blushed red.

"I'll be needing some cash for my trip," she told him while he was still trying to decide how to react.

"Where are you going?" he asked when he'd regained some composure.

"Romania," Josephine said flatly, as though she were taking a trip to Montgomery.

"Romania?" He stared at her as though she'd suggested a trip to the moon.

"It's a country in eastern Europe. The other side of Hungary."

"Yes! I know where Romania is… basically. But why are you going there?"

"My father asked me to take my grandfather's ashes and spread them in the Carpathian Mountains," she said simply.

Robertson's mouth made more fish-out-of-water movements. "Why in the world would your father ask you to do that?"

"It was a promise he'd made to his father."

"A man in your father's condition can get all kinds of funny ideas. You can't take a request like that seriously."

"My father was in his right mind when he asked me to do this," Josephine said, not totally sure this was the truth.

"Of course, but when you're dying… you… get ideas. I remember my grandmother wanted us all to sing hymns by her bedside during her last days. A person facing death has… fears. Talk to Father Mullen. He'll be able to advise you better than me."

Josephine had no intention of going to Father Mullen. The priest's opinion that women should not do anything other than run the household was well known.

"I'll think about it," she lied. "Now, here is what I'm going to need." She laid out a piece of paper with several figures written on it.

"Who is going with you?" Robertson asked, ignoring the paper.

"Grace will accompany me," Josephine answered, though she hadn't yet brought the subject up with the opinionated maid.

"That's one thing, but what about a proper chaperone? Grace is… black. She won't be able to enter restaurants and other establishments. You can't eat alone. Seriously, Josie, you can't do this."

"Seriously, Mr. Robertson, I am going to do this. This is not a pleasure trip to Saratoga. I'll be eating my meals in my room while traveling and Grace can eat with me. I have thought this out. My plan is to go to Romania by the most direct and expedient route. Once at my grandfather's village, I'll spread his ashes and return."

Josephine knew Mr. Robertson was right to some extent. She would have to be discreet to prevent any trouble, but it was not unheard of for a middle-aged woman to travel with her servant. Middle-aged, she thought. Am I really middle-aged? Thirty-five was not old, but she was very close to being labeled a spinster.

"Still, that is a very long trip."

"When we arrive, I'll be met by relatives," Josephine said, hoping that it was true. She had found a few letters from distant cousins that her father had kept. She hadn't been able to read them since they were in Romanian, but she'd been able to discern that they were from family.

"Have you talked to Bobby?" Robertson asked.

Josephine sighed. Robertson was clearly floundering about for any lifeline in this argument. Bobby was Robert Tucker, a local sheriff's deputy who had courted her off and on since they were in school together. He was a nice man, but he didn't seem to understand that while she liked him, she didn't want to bind their lives together in marriage. Ever.

"Bobby Tucker has nothing to do with this," she said bluntly, tired of humoring Robertson. "Provide me with what I've asked for, and I'll think about the objections you've raised."

"If you are determined to do this, then at least let me see if I can find someone else to act as a chaperone."

"You may do as you wish," she said and purposely slid the note with her proposed travel expenses across his desk.

CHAPTER TWO

Josephine returned home two hours later. She'd gotten the money and sent several telegrams, including one to an agent requesting passage on a ship from New York to France.

She was drenched in sweat as she entered the house. Though it was only early April, it was already too warm to wear a heavy black woolen dress, but she didn't mind suffering to mourn her father.

"Grace, would you come in here?" Josephine called out.

Grace was removing dead flowers from the arrangements that had been left in the house after the funeral. "Yes, ma'am."

She followed Josephine into the front parlor, which still held Mr. Nicolson's bed.

"Have a seat," Josephine said, remaining standing while Grace, uncertain, sat on the edge of the sofa.

"I need a favor of you." Josephine hesitated, trying to decide the best approach.

Meanwhile, Grace's mind had raced ahead to the worst case scenario and was seeing a future without a job or the chance of getting one.

"No, Miss Josephine, I've got to work for you. Just 'cus your daddy's gone... I don't know what's the matter, but I need this job."

Josephine held out her hand, trying to quiet her. "I'm not firing you. Nothing of the sort. How could you think that?"

'Cause white folk are crazy, the voice in Grace's head answered. What she said to Josephine was: "With nobody havin' any money anymore, I thought maybe you were broke like everyone else." Grace wondered what Josephine wanted from her.

"I want you to accompany me to Romania," Josephine blurted out.

"Roman what? You talkin' the other side of the world?" Grace asked, astonished at the idea. She'd once traveled as far as Atlanta, but the trip had been an ordeal with many dangers for a black family traveling through strange towns and counties. They hadn't known the local rules or where it was safe for them to stop for food, fuel or to use the restroom. She remembered her father being so nervous that he had lashed out at anyone who'd asked him a question.

"Not quite the other side of the world, but the other side of the ocean. A long way. But I need your help. Papa made a request before he died. I can't do this alone."

"But can't you go with some white folks?" Grace couldn't understand why Josephine wanted her to go.

"No. I can't go with a man, and I don't have the time or patience to go with a woman my age."

The latter was certainly the truth. Most of Josephine's friends were married and their husbands would never let them be gone for weeks at a time. She knew a few unmarried teachers, but the women at the local school who were young enough to make the trip would be as much, if not more, trouble than her other option, which was to take an elderly woman who'd need an extra bag just for her medicines. "No, I need you to go with me. I'll provide a travel bonus for your trouble."

Bonus. Grace liked the sound of that word. She lived in a small house on the dirt street behind the Nicolson house. The street was little more than a large alley lined with neat and tidy shotgun houses where the servants and workmen for Sumter's rich and comfortable lived. The Depression had fallen hard on the small community of working men and women. Grace's little green house was in need of some serious repairs. She'd given her brother what little money she'd saved up to help his family after he'd lost his job at the railroad yard.

"I don't mean to be forward none, but how much would this bonus money be?" Grace asked carefully, not wanting to scare the golden goose away.

"Your current salary is eight dollars a week, which is above average for your job," Josephine said unnecessarily. Grace already knew she was being paid more than twice what a lot of her friends were getting.

"Yes, ma'am. Mr. Andre was always very kind to me," Grace said, thinking that spreading some honey wouldn't hurt.

"We'll be gone for possibly as long as a month," Josephine said, calculating what a generous bonus would be. "Let's say, on top of your regular salary, you'll receive an additional forty dollars."

Grace was amazed. She wanted to act uncertain, but that much extra money would allow her to fix up her house. She'd get her brother to do the work. He needed something to keep him busy.

"You sure we don't need more than a month?" she asked, warming to this whole idea of international travel.

"I think a month will be long enough. You'll need some items from the dry goods store, and I can loan you one of our suitcases. Maybe some new clothes," Josephine told her and watched as suspicion was replaced by excitement in Grace's eyes.

The next two days were spent in preparation for the trip. Josephine realized early on that Grace had no experience with travel and needed advice on most aspects of packing.

Josephine had accompanied Grace to the small clothing store that catered to the middle-class black community in town. Grace's status was raised in the eyes of the shopkeeper when she was accompanied by her boss, who brought in cash money. Everyone was all smiles by the time they left with packages piled high.

Josephine had already purchased their train tickets at the depot for travel on a first-class carriage via the Southern and Atlantic Railway to New York. From there, her New York agent had secured them tickets for the transatlantic crossing on RMS *Majestic*.

The evening before they were to leave, Josephine was upstairs in her room, trying to decide what and how to pack. She envied Grace, who wasn't required by convention to have a dozen different outfits. Even though this was the 1930s and women like Amelia Earhart were able to get away with dressing in practical clothing, on board a ship and while staying in hotels, Josephine didn't have many options. Josephine had been assured that the captain of the British ship would be more than willing to confine her to her room for the duration of the voyage if she wasn't wearing what they considered to be appropriate dress.

She had just finished cramming everything into two trunks and a Pullman bag when Grace came up the stairs and knocked on the door.

"No sense hidin'. He's not going away this time!" Grace shouted.

With a sigh, Josephine opened the door.

"You told him I couldn't see him right now?" Josephine asked and Grace frowned.

"Didn't you tell me to tell him that? He's not budgin'. Mr. Bobby says he's gonna be on that front porch until you come out."

"He'll get tired and go away."

"I don't think so. He's got a blanket roll and everything."

"Fine! I'll just have to deal with this," Josephine said petulantly and moved past Grace.

"You better put on some clothes!" Grace said and Josephine realized that she was still wearing the robe she'd donned after trying on various outfits.

Ten minutes later, composed, Josephine opened the front door.

"Bobby, Grace told you I don't have time this evening," she said, going on the attack.

"Josie, what are you doing? Mr. Robertson told me you were off on some foolish journey to Italy or some place."

Bobby Tucker, just a year older than Josephine and still boyish-looking, had always had a crush on her. She'd tried to get him to move on, but he had a well deserved reputation for being one of the most stubborn men in the county, which was saying a lot. His competition included Old Man Floyd, who'd stood out in a half-plowed field for two days waiting out a mule who was determined not to plow another foot of ground. In the end, the field had been plowed and one hungry mule had learned a hard lesson.

"I'm going to Romania to spread my grandfather's ashes."

"That's crazy. If you want to go to Europe, there are folks you could travel with. Going by yourself is dangerous."

On the one hand, Josephine really wanted to slam the door in his face, but on the other she knew his concern was real. As well as being stubborn, he was kindhearted to a fault. He still had a scar on his arm from saving an old stray dog from a shed that had caught fire.

"I'm taking Grace with me. I told Robertson I'd send a telegram a couple of times a week to let him know my progress. After all, this isn't the dark ages."

"You'll be in a foreign country without any friends, Josie. No matter how you look at it, that's dangerous."

"I've got family in Romania. I won't be all alone." In truth, she had no idea whether she'd be able to locate any members of her family or not, but she had the names from the letters she'd found in her father's desk.

"I don't know about that, but, look, give me a week and

I'll find someone to go with you."

"No," she said firmly.

"But Josie…"

"No! I'll be back in a month. People travel all over the world all the time and they don't disappear or get attacked. If it makes you feel better, I'll send you a telegram at the same time I send one to Robertson."

Bobby narrowed his eyes and stared hard at her. He knew her well enough to know he couldn't push things any further.

"Okay, but you got to let us know where you are, where you're going, how and when. And if we don't get a telegram, I'm coming to look for you," he said with a determination that carried his word and his honor.

Josephine had no doubt Bobby would be on her trail in an instant if he thought something was wrong. If she was honest with herself, knowing that she would have the cavalry in reserve if something did go wrong was comforting.

"If I give you a little kiss on the cheek, will you take it the wrong way?" she asked him.

He blushed and leaned down. She gave him a quick peck and he reached out to take her hand gently in his.

"You have any problem, you just let me know and I'll come runnin' or flyin' or swimmin'. Whatever I have to do to get there."

"I know that, Bobby."

After an awkward pause, Josephine told him that he had to go so she could finish packing and get some rest. As she shut the door behind his retreating back, she wondered if she was doing the right thing. Not just about the trip, but about Bobby. He was a good man, there was no question about that. And she'd seen enough of life to know that good men weren't as common as one would hope.

There had been a day when she was sixteen, down by the river, when Bobby had kissed her for the first time and she'd felt all the goosebumps and wild excitement that you're supposed to feel when someone you love kisses you. But the feeling had faded years ago. Now she just felt comfortable with him. He was a man she could count on. Was that enough? *Damn it, I can't think about all this right now. We've got to be at the train station by nine*, she reminded herself and started back up the stairs.

Three steps up the stairs and she remembered the one thing she couldn't forget. She came back down and went into the front parlor. The vase with her grandfather's ashes stared back at her from the mantel. With everything else, she hadn't taken the time to think how she was going to transport the ashes. Taking the vase would be impractical.

How much ash is there? she wondered.

She lifted the vase up off the mantel. It was heavy, but mostly because of the vase itself. Josephine peered inside. The vase was over halfway full with maybe a quart and a half of ash. Thinking about her options, she set the vase back on the mantel and noticed a small book that had been behind the vase.

The book was handwritten in Romanian. As she flipped through the leather-bound journal, she recognized the names of her grandfather and grandmother. Taking the book, she went into her father's library and found the old Romanian/English dictionary that she'd tried and failed to master as a child when she'd wanted to impress her grandfather.

With both the journal and the dictionary firmly in hand, she went upstairs and packed them in her Pullman case so she would have them close by while they traveled. Then she yelled down to Grace to dig up a large mason jar. Once she had the mason jar in hand, she filled it with her grandfather's ashes.

"Whoever heard of such a thing?" Grace asked, watching the ash shift from the vase to the jar. In spite of herself, she was fascinated by the dark grey material. "How do they do it? I mean, have they got a big old fire pit or an oven or something?"

"Honestly, I don't know. I guess an oven. Papa didn't say

much about it after he came back." She was concentrating on not spilling the ashes.

At last the jar was filled. There was about half a cup of her grandfather's remains still inside the vase. "Sorry, but part of you is going to stay in Alabama," she said to the ashes.

Carefully screwing the lid down on the mason jar, she debated which suitcase the jar would travel in. Reluctantly, she decided that it needed to go into her Pullman case. She'd seen trunks fall off of luggage trucks and the thought of the jar breaking and her clothes covered in ash wasn't appealing.

CHAPTER THREE

Josephine and Grace made it to New York in two days' time, a bit rougher for wear. Amazed at the sights whizzing past the window, Grace hadn't slept much on the train.

For her part, Josephine had spent hours on the train going through her grandfather's journal. The grammar was lost on her, but by defining as many words as she could with the dictionary, she was able to make some sense of it.

The journal had been started in the spring of 1865 while her grandfather was living in the village of Satul de Dealuri Verzi high in the Carpathian Mountains. The words *boala* and *moarte* were repeated over and over. Sickness and death. The words for "fear" and "unknown" were also repeated along with a great many names. Some of the dead were *copii*, children. The more Josephine translated, the more she understood the sorrow that the little leather-bound book represented. She wasn't sorry when they reached New York and she could put the diary away for a while.

Josephine had never been to New York and was as gobsmacked by the size as Grace was. Luckily, at the last minute Josephine had relented and allowed Mr. Robertson to contact a friend of his in the city who met them and took them to their hotel. From there they would take a cab to the terminal where they would board the *Majestic*.

While Josephine spent time with Robertson's friend, Parker Reed, and his family, Grace walked around the hotel and talked with any black people she could find. One of the cooks invited Grace to a club in Harlem, but she was too timid to accept. At church, she'd heard wild stories about the evil men who lurked around jazz clubs. The smoking bellboys told her that "There ain't no Prohibition in no club in Harlem." That confirmed her decision to stay away because Grace's Aunt May had told her a hundred times that liquor and bastard babies went together like molasses and biscuits.

Meanwhile, Parker and his wife were able to talk Josephine into entering a speakeasy. She couldn't believe the scene that unfolded before her eyes. The noise, smoke, music, smells and clothes alone would have overwhelmed her, but when added to the looks and winks from the men and the language these people were using in public, Josephine found herself both fascinated and repulsed. She took a look at her hosts and wondered if Mr. Robertson had any idea where his friends were taking her.

After two days in the city, both women were looking forward to a week on the ship to recover. The hustle and bustle of the dock and the first sight of the *Majestic* tied to her moorings just added to the sense that they were out of their depth. The ship towered above them as they tried to push their way through the people and cargo lining the dock.

As they settled in on the ship, Josephine felt a little disappointment at the fact that Grace couldn't go everywhere with her. For Josephine, Grace's race was less important than the fact that she was a familiar face in a sea of strangers. But at least Grace was allowed to stay in a room off of her first-class cabin. The ship was designed with the wealthy traveler in mind, and it was expected that the well-off would travel with their own domestic help.

"I don't mind, Miss Josephine. I'm fine takin' my meals

in here. After that city, I'm glad for a little peace and quiet. I've got my Bible, and I promised Aunt May I'd read it every day," Grace said, lying only a little.

For Grace, the restrictions on her movements were a bit harder to take here because she didn't know all of the rules and kept being reminded that she was considered a lesser person. Of course, she'd also seen some folks who were whiter than white being shooed away from the first-class areas. There were lines drawn for race and lines drawn between the rich and poor. At least she was traveling with a rich person.

Poor black people just have no chance in this world, she thought. A stab of fear and sadness pierced her heart as she remembered her brother, who was now jobless with two children and a wife to support. She'd told them they could move into her house while she was gone. Grace had a small attic room in the Nicolson house that she used when she needed to work long hours. She'd stayed there most of the time during the last three months of Mr. Nicolson's illness so that she could help nurse him. *I could ask Miss Josephine if I can stay there while Ronnie gets back up on his feet*, Grace thought as she opened the Bible to her favorite Psalm.

After her first day onboard, Josephine made friends with several of the other passengers and even spent time talking with several of the ship's officers. There was a pall over the crew, who knew the *Majestic's* days were numbered. The economic times had hit the transatlantic trade hard. The White Star Line and the Cunard Line would soon be forced to merge and it would only be a matter of time until the *Majestic* was taken out of service.

After a calm and uneventful voyage, they arrived on time in Cherbourg, France. Standing on the pier with her luggage and looking out at a strange city, Josephine could hear dozens of people speaking different languages. *And I've only finished the second leg of my journey*, she thought. The number of miles that still lay in front of her were almost overwhelming. *What was I thinking?* she wondered.

She looked over at Grace, whose face reflected everything that Josephine was feeling. *Having dragged her along on this quixotic adventure, I can't let her know how terrified I am*, Josephine told herself.

"We need to get a cab to our hotel," Josephine said, just as a young man with a ridiculous mustache stepped up and introduced himself. At least she assumed he was introducing himself. The man was spewing forth a novel's worth of French in a matter of seconds. He pointed back toward a taxi cab that had a few more dents in it than seemed reasonable.

"Hotel du Mont," Josephine said several times. The man finally realized they didn't speak French and nodded, smiling. He picked up two of their trunks with an almost herculean strength and hustled them to his cab. Grace picked up the two remaining bags while Josephine walked with her Pullman case. The man came trotting back and took the two bags from a surprised Grace, winking at her as he did so.

"Well, I never!" Grace said, trying to sound scandalized, but looking like a child who'd just been given an ice cream cone.

At the hotel, Josephine managed to communicate with the concierge, who agreed to purchase the train tickets they needed for the next part of the journey. While Josephine was discussing their plans with the concierge, Grace stood waiting by their luggage. The manager of the hotel appeared at her side and asked in passable English if she needed help. At first, Grace thought that he wanted her to move to a more inconspicuous location. She was used to white people not wanting black folk cluttering up their establishments. But something about the way he asked was odd. She took a chance and looked up at him to see him looking back, attentive and interested.

"Has Madam registered? Do you need the bellman?"

"No, sir. I'm waitin' on Miss Josephine. She's made all the arrangements," Grace told him, not knowing what to do with her eyes.

"Very good, Madam. Just let us know if we can be of service."

Grace almost fell over. Never in her thirty-eight years had a white person offered to be of service to her. After he left, Grace remembered her daddy and her uncles talking about being in France during the Great War. They would shake their heads and ask each other why they'd ever come home. That would lead them to talking about what they called the "parlayvu" girls. That's when her mother and aunts would give them dirty looks and tell them that, if they were going to act that way, then they may as well *have* stayed in France. Now Grace was seeing what they had seen, and it was as if she'd been locked in a windowless room all of her life and someone suddenly opened the door to a world of light and color.

Josephine and Grace spent only one night in Cherbourg before boarding the train for Paris and beyond. The route would take them through Germany and Austria to a small town in Romania called Curtea de Arges. Before they left the hotel, Josephine made arrangements for their two large trunks to be stored in Cherbourg until their return.

As the train rocked through the French countryside, Josephine continued to work her way through her grandfather's journal. She'd reached the halfway point and was coming across another word. *Monstru.*

What kind of monster? Josephine wondered. The tight handwriting was difficult to decipher, increasingly blotted with ink spots and more crossed-out words as she went along. She could almost feel the fear that her grandfather must have been experiencing as the village's dead piled up.

Focused on the journal, Josephine was startled when she heard Grace gasp loudly. Looking up, she saw Grace staring out of the window. Following her gaze, Josephine saw the scars left by the Great War that had ended a mere fifteen years before, leaving thirty-eight million dead and wounded.

The land was still deeply disfigured by the brutal war. They passed miles and miles of artillery craters and abandoned trenches that were still too dangerous to be reworked into farmland. Every few miles, they saw burial grounds filled with row upon row of knee-high white crosses.

"How much farther we got to go?" Grace asked as they passed signs counting down the miles to Deutschland.

"We still have to travel through Germany and Austria. A day, maybe. Depending on how often the train stops and if we're delayed." They'd been lucky so far, with good weather and not too many other travelers.

"They don't look like they're much better off than we are," Grace observed as she looked out at the French farmers and villagers. The country was still reeling from economic depression after a war that had left too many men and women broken in body and spirit.

As the train screeched to a halt at the German border, Josephine looked out at the customs station. The black, white and red striped flag of the German Weimar Republic still flew over the border office, and Hindenburg, now elderly and doddering, was still president. But all the talk was about the chancellor appointed by Hindenburg earlier that year. It was clear Adolf Hitler was taking control of the country. As they traveled through Germany, there was no doubt that the country looked more prosperous and optimistic than France.

"That is one ugly flag," Grace said as they passed a house flying the banner of the National Socialist Party—a black swastika in a white circle on a red field. Josephine felt a cold chill go over her. The flag conjured up something dark and ominous. It was odd, since before this she'd always associated the swastika with the Boy Scouts and their meetings at the local school. But seeing it now seemed like a throwback to a darker age.

The differences between France and Germany had been stark, but when they came to Austria, the only things that made it clear they were leaving one country and entering another were the signs and the customs agents.

Austria was breathtakingly beautiful. The white-capped hills were a brilliant green against the deep blue of the spring sky. Neither woman could take their eyes off of the flickering landscape as it passed the train's windows.

"I never seen anything this beautiful," Grace exclaimed. For a moment, in the excitement of the journey and the shared wonders they were seeing, Grace let her guard down and felt as if she were talking to a friend.

"Me neither. The mountains make me feel very small," Josephine said, looking out at the towering landscape.

Eventually, Josephine went back to the journal. She wanted to make her way through the entire book before they had to travel by bus or hired car.

In the story unfolding in the diary, her grandfather had contacted someone called a *vanator*, a hunter, to save the village. He described the arrival of the hunter as a big event. But a page later her grandfather noted that what the hunter wanted was too much. *Too much what?* Josephine wondered. Also, her grandfather mentioned his brothers. *Brothers?* Josephine could not remember her father ever mentioning that he had any uncles.

The words in the diary become even more dense and hard to read. A hunt. Brothers. The hunter. *Mort. Mort. Mort. Mort.* Four times dead. Soon she reached the part where her grandfather left Romania for America. Here she saw the word for revenge. "Someday revenge."

Josephine closed the journal. Many of the words and much of the meaning were lost in her inability to speak Romanian, but she understood that her grandfather had worked with the hunter and his brothers to fight something he had considered to be a great evil. Eventually only he had survived, along with their nemesis.

Josephine knew that it must have been a massive wound to his pride to have to flee an enemy that had killed his brothers. She now understood that her grandfather had wanted his ashes returned as a final act of defiance in the face of the *monstru*. She felt vindicated in her decision to impulsively pack up and embark on this trip. The gesture needed to be made and, if she'd hesitated, the weight of everyday problems would have overshadowed the need to fulfill this obligation to a man whose decisions had made her life possible.

Rain began to fall as they crossed the border into Romania. Josephine tried not to take it as an omen. The train rattled through small towns and villages. The scenes passing by the windows couldn't have looked much different a hundred years earlier.

"I hope we got a dry bed to sleep in," Grace said. "Don't look like they got any hotels in this country." The rain had dampened both their moods.

At two o'clock in the afternoon, the train's brakes screamed as they slid into the depot in Curtea de Arges. The town was on flat ground alongside the River Arges. Josephine, Grace and their luggage were put down on the station platform while new passengers boarded the train for Budapest. After a few attempts, Josephine found a man who spoke passable English.

"We need to go into the mountains," she explained.

"Yes, yes. Carriage. I have a cousin; he will take you." The man smiled and nodded.

"A bus? Maybe a car?"

"No, no, too wet. Much rain this season. Only horses can make it up the road into the mountains." He smiled. "Where are you going?"

"A small village north of Capatineni. The village is called Satul de Dealuri Verzi. Near a place called Cetatea Blasko."

"My cousin he will take you to Capataneni, but no farther." The man was frowning now.

"But we need to go to Satul de Dealuri Verzi."

"We find my cousin. He'll be in the stable. Come, come."

He picked up one of their bags and yelled to a young

man loitering by the station door. Words passed between them. The only word Josephine recognized was *leu*, the Romanian dollar. The younger man came over grudgingly and lifted the other two bags.

The streets were cobblestone and covered in mud and manure. As they followed the men, Grace and Josephine had to hang onto each other to keep from slipping and falling. The livery stable rang with the clanging of the blacksmith fitting shoes to a black-and-white draft horse.

They were left on the sidewalk outside the livery as the man they'd come with went inside, shouting for his cousin. A few minutes later, a large man with rough hands that looked more like bear paws came out and looked at the women and their luggage. He twirled his mustache with more dexterity than Josephine would have thought possible with his sausage fingers.

The man and his cousin went into negotiations that involved much fast talking followed by moments of contemplation... followed by more fast talking.

Finally the man who had brought them said, "My cousin has to wait for his horses to be shod. But he'll take you there. Leaving first light." He quoted a price that seemed high to Josephine. She thought about the pros and cons of haggling, but decided she was really in no position to do so.

"Is there a hotel near here?"

"A fine establishment. My uncle will treat you very well. My aunt, an excellent cook."

The man beamed. He spoke Romanian to his cousin, whose face also burst into a smile as he started to nod his head up and down. Josephine realized she was having to put herself and Grace into the hands of men who could be crooks, or worse. But what choice did she have?

"In for a penny, in for a pound," she muttered to herself. "Take us to your uncle's hotel."

Surprisingly, the inn *was* comfortable. Small and cozy, it had a tavern on the ground floor. They had to walk through the tables and past the bar to get to the stairs that led up to their bedroom.

Josephine and Grace, without conferring, had come to the same conclusion. They wanted one room. Josephine's mind went back to her years as a schoolgirl when she'd gone on a binge of gothic romances. The heroine's dangerous adventure always started at a strange inn on the way to a dark and brooding manor house. But the laughter, enthusiastic conversation and shouting from the tavern helped to put her at ease. The people here seemed to be genuinely happy. There didn't seem to be any dark and ominous secret hanging over these folk.

The bed was a huge four-poster with a feather mattress and an extravagant number of quilts. The explanation for the amount of covers became apparent as the sun went down and the temperature with it. No one offered to light the round, ornate stove in the corner.

"If there's some wood, I'd get that thing goin'," Grace said, staring at the cold stove.

"Never mind. We'll be leaving first thing in the morning."

Josephine had been able to communicate a little with the innkeeper, and he'd assured her he would see that she was awakened with breakfast at first light. He had also promised that his son would be there to take their luggage over to the livery.

The dinner that night was very good—hearty helpings of beef stew and spicy biscuits. Josephine hoped their journey would continue to be blessed with good fortune. More than ever, she knew she was taking a huge risk. Her home and friends were far away. She and Grace were truly strangers in a strange land.

Josephine was comforted by the prayers Grace said as she kneeled down by the bed. When Grace got up, she looked uncertain. Josephine had already gotten into bed and burrowed down under the quilts.

"Are you sure it's okay? I could sleep on that old thing," Grace said, pointing to a large ornate bench. "A couple of blankets and a pillow, I'll be fine."

"Don't be silly. We're going to need each other to keep from freezing to death."

Grace clambered into the bed and settled herself under the blankets. Josephine blew out the candle and the women listened to the jolly sounds rising up from below. Both managed a few hours of sleep before there was a polite knocking on the door.

Within an hour, they were walking to the livery behind a young man who somehow managed to carry all of their luggage. In front of the livery was an old-fashioned mail carriage with a four-horse team of draft horses. The rig looked suitable for the roughest terrain, making Josephine relax a bit.

There were several other people standing around the carriage, including a short man wearing a khaki military uniform. He had enough gold metal on his shoulder straps for Josephine to feel safe in assuming that he was an officer.

As they drew close, the man turned and shouted something to the innkeeper's son carrying their luggage. As the boy hustled over to the carriage, the man greeted Josephine.

"You must be the English ladies," he said with a Romanian accent. "Captain Vladimir Petran at your service." He tried to click his heels, but the muddy road made it a hollow gesture.

"American, actually. I'm Josephine Nicolson and this is Grace Dunn." She had almost said "my servant" after introducing Grace. Of course, in America she would have never introduced her at all. Here, the old rules seemed silly.

"A pleasure," he said with a smile, which highlighted a wicked scar that ran from the corner of his eye to his mouth. He noticed Josephine's glance and touched it. "I spent years being embarrassed by this, but every day I find myself learning to appreciate the fact I have such a prominent reminder of my good luck."

"The war?"

"I was advancing with my regiment across a field toward the enemy line when an artillery shell went off next to me. I was thrown unconscious onto razor wire. All of the men who went forward from that point were wounded severely. Compared to them, this," he said, rubbing the scar, "is a small price."

"Are you traveling with us?"

"Yes. It was most fortuitous that your driver announced he had a fare going into the mountains. This couple is also going," he said, pointing to a man and a woman who looked like they were barely out of their teens. From their expressions, they obviously didn't understand English. The couple seemed particularly intrigued by Grace. The young man spoke to the captain. It was clear he was asking about the maid.

"What is it?" Josephine asked.

The captain smiled at Josephine, but spoke to Grace. "The boy wants to know if you are a Nubian or a Moor."

"You tell him I'm from Alabama and I'm a Christian. I'm not some heathen," Grace said.

The captain smiled and spoke to the young couple. They smiled and nodded without taking their eyes off of Grace.

Before they could say more, the driver came out of the livery and walked around the horses, checking their harnesses before telling the five of them to get inside the carriage. While they'd been talking, all of the luggage had been precariously perched on the roof of the carriage by another man.

Josephine and Grace had never ridden in a stagecoach and it had been years since either had been in any type of carriage. Once everyone was seated, they were all practically touching elbows and knees. The couple sat on the same side as Grace while the captain and Josephine sat across from them.

"Where are you going?" Josephine asked him.

"I'm surveying for a new road through the mountains. The government wants to improve all the passes."

"You aren't doing that by yourself?"

"No. I'm authorized to hire or conscript whoever I need to get the job done. Tell me, why are two Americans headed into the Carpathian Mountains?"

"I'm visiting my grandfather's village. He came to America in the last century."

"What village?"

"It's near Capataneni. The name is Satul de Dealuri Verzi."

At the mention of the village, the couple became visibly upset. They spoke to each other in hushed tones. Finally, the man leaned toward Captain Petran and spoke to him. The conversation went back and forth for a few minutes before the captain, looking grim, turned to Josephine.

"I'm so sorry to tell you, but according to these folks the village is no longer there. It was abandoned long ago," Petran said sympathetically as the couple watched expectantly.

"They are from the area?"

The captain relayed the question. The young man gave a brief answer.

"They live farther up in the mountains, but have family that live nearby."

"What happened to it?" Josephine asked. Her inner sense told her that the village's abandonment must have had to do with the events in her grandfather's journal.

After a brief exchange with the couple, the captain turned back to Josephine. "They say that it was before they were born, but they know many people died. Perhaps an illness."

Everyone in the carriage remembered the Spanish Flu epidemic. It had spread around the world as soldiers returned from the battlefields at the end of the Great War. Tens of millions had died. Before that, it wasn't uncommon for typhoid or polio to run rampant through a town or region. But Josephine had read enough in her grandfather's journal to think the plague that had devastated the village had been something much more tangible.

CHAPTER FOUR

For the rest of the day, everyone seemed lost in their own thoughts as the carriage swayed and bumped over the rough road that was deeply rutted from the rains. A stop for lunch and to rest the horses ended too soon for Josephine and Grace. The carriage ride was bone-jarring and exhausting.

"We'll be at Capataneni before nightfall," Captain Petran told the women.

Despite his encouragement, it was still five more hours before the carriage came to a stop at the largest inn in the town. Entering the tavern, both women realized that their stay was not going to be as comfortable as the night before, but they were so tired that anything resembling a bed would be welcomed.

They shared a hearty stew with the captain, then retreated to their room. It was neat and held two twin beds, but little else in the way of comfort. The quilts were old and worn and the mattresses were cotton ticking stuffed with straw.

Now that they were in the mountains, the temperature dropped more quickly than the night before. Trying to ignore the cold, Josephine lay in bed wondering what she should do. *Is the village really gone? Could the couple have been mistaken?* Captain Petran had promised to stay a day in

Capataneni and help her find any relatives that might be living in the area. *Maybe I should just scatter the ashes here and start the long journey home,* was her last thought before falling asleep.

A night's rest and the sight of the sun streaming through the window helped to brighten Josephine's mood. Downstairs at the table, the captain was eating *mamaliga*, a cornmeal-based porridge, and drinking a dark tea.

"After you went to bed, I made some inquiries. I sent a messenger to tell a man who may be your cousin that you are here. According to the locals, he lives only a couple miles away. They could be back as early as noon."

Josephine helped herself to a bowl of porridge and a cup of tea. "Thank you. I'm very grateful for your help."

"I'm impressed that you show respect for your grandfather's wishes. Romanians put great store in our elders. He must have been a great man."

"He was… an unusual man."

"Tough. Look at us. Our skin is like leather. Romanians are able to weather the storms when others are swept away by them."

"He was definitely a tough man. Always kind to me. Not always as kind to my father."

"Ha, we are hardest on our sons. For thousands of years, to be Romanian was to fight. Real fighting, not like the last war. That was slaughter. I saw officers kill themselves rather than order their men to die. I was lucky. I was in the engineers. Better, but even I had to order men to work while the enemy picked them off like targets at a country fair."

"We were lucky."

"Yes, by the time the Americans arrived, the war had been decided. Though your army fought well. I've been to America."

"Really?"

"Texas. I came to observe military maneuvers. Very impressive. Texas reminded me of Romania. The men are like us, leathery and tough." He laughed.

Josephine liked the man. He seemed able to overcome the darkness he'd seen during the war. Plenty of the returning soldiers back home hadn't been able to return to their old lives so easily. She wondered how often Captain Petran saw the ghosts of his friends and comrades.

"Would you look at a journal that my grandfather wrote? It's in Romanian. I've done the best I could with a dictionary, but…"

An hour later, Captain Petran came to Josephine, holding the diary and looking at her as though she had played a joke on him.

"Romanian peasants are a superstitious lot. I'm afraid your grandfather was too gullible."

"I know that he talks about some sort of monster, but…"

"He says there was a blood-sucking monster stalking his village, and that he and some other men went out one day to kill this creature. They all ended up dead except for your grandfather, who then fled the country." The captain sounded very dismissive.

"You think they were imagining the deaths in the village?" This sounded ridiculous to Josephine, though she had to admit that the idea of a blood-drinking monster was pretty crazy.

"Eighty years ago, there could have been wolves or a bear preying on the locals. Possibly even a madman—there are plenty of humans who are capable of committing atrocities. But I don't believe in mythical monsters."

"That young couple said the village was abandoned?"

"Probably because of a series of misfortunes. Like I said, peasants can be scared of their own shadows. A couple of murders and then an epidemic, next thing you know, the villagers are talking about a curse and moving away." He shrugged.

"Maybe my cousin will know more," Josephine suggested.

"Perhaps."

They sat for a while in silence before Josephine excused herself and went back to the room to make sure Grace was all right.

"I woke up and didn't know where I was. I thought I was sleepin' on a bed of rocks till I saw that it was only this old mattress," Grace said. "I don't think I'm ever going to leave Semmes County again."

"You should go down and have breakfast."

"Where are we goin' today?" Grace asked, half scared of the answer.

"I don't know yet," Josephine answered honestly.

As they came down the stairs, Josephine saw a man sitting with Captain Petran. There was something oddly familiar about him. The captain stood and the man followed suit.

"Miss Nicolson, this is Constantin Antonescu." Captain Petran introduced the man who looked uncomfortable, but managed to bow somewhat awkwardly. Constantin was dressed in a linen shirt and brown woolen coat and pants. His boots had seen more barns than sidewalks. "I'm afraid he doesn't speak much English."

The captain spoke to the man in Romanian for a few moments. "He says that the family is pleased to meet the granddaughter of Grigore Nicolescu. He apologizes that his home is so humble, otherwise he would invite you to stay there as his guest."

"Tell him not to worry. I'm from a small town in America. Many of my friends are farmers." Then she added, "Tell him the smell of horse manure doesn't bother me."

The captain smiled a little and relayed the message to Constantin, who smiled broadly at Josephine.

"I'm a little at a loss, Captain. I was hoping some of my family would speak English. That seems like a naïve idea now. But when I was planning my trip…" She let the thought trail off.

"I would be happy to serve as your translator for the next couple of days," he said, clicking his heels.

"I wouldn't want to keep you from your survey work," Josephine said, pleased that he had offered.

"I have time to do both. If for even one moment I thought that my commission would prevent me from helping a beautiful woman, I would resign immediately." He snapped his fingers.

Josephine smiled. Between the clicking of his heels and the snapping of his fingers, the man reminded her of the crabs at the beach. *But much nicer*, she thought.

Captain Petran turned back to Constantin and spoke for a few moments. "We can ride with him back to his house. It is only a couple of miles from here, and he has a wagon."

"That would be fine. Let me talk to my… companion for a moment." There were folks back in Semmes County who would have been scandalized to hear her refer to Grace as her companion.

She walked over to the table where Grace was eating porridge and bread. In the small room, Grace had been able to overhear everything they'd been saying, so Josephine didn't have to go into great detail.

"Grace, would you mind staying here while I visit my relative's farm?"

"Oh, no, ma'am. Stayin' put for a day isn't gonna bother me at all," she said with sincerity and gusto.

Once at the farm, Josephine looked at her other cousins and realized that Constantin had looked so familiar because he, like the rest of them, was family. This obvious truth created an almost instant bond with these people. It was odd that they could be so foreign yet remind her so much of her life and home.

One young man in particular looked a lot like her father when he was young. Josephine remembered an old photograph that hung in her father's office, showing him holding a hunting rifle and standing with several other men she knew from Sumter. His look of youthful enthusiasm and grit was reflected in the boy, Gheorghe.

Josephine and the captain spent the day with the family. Most of the men had work to do, but they would relieve each other so they could all come and see their unusual visitors. While there seemed to be a natural affinity between the family and Josephine, they all seemed as suspicious of the captain as he was of them. She would catch them giving him sideways glances and sometimes whispering. *Is it because he's an officer? Or a difference of class? Or is it because he comes from a different part of Romania?* she wondered.

When Josephine talked about her grandfather, everyone would get quiet as Captain Petran translated. Questions about the events that had caused him to flee to America were met with headshakes and assurances that no one knew anything about it. Josephine encouraged the captain to press them, which was only met with more vigorous denials. She was told that everyone had simply moved away from the village. After much back and forth, the captain was able to draw a crude map that showed the village in relation to the town of Capataneni and the family's homestead.

Toward late afternoon, Elena Nicolescu, the elderly family matriarch, invited Josephine to stay for the night. Josephine demurred, saying she needed to get back to her friend at the inn, but she promised to come back the next day. She wanted one last chance to see them before heading home. She had originally thought she might spend days or a week with her distant relatives, but seeing them, she realized that her presence was a disruption to their lives. A day or two was a pleasant distraction; more than that seemed to risk unforeseen consequences.

On the way back to the inn in Constantin's wagon, Josephine told the captain, "I want to go to the village and spread my grandfather's ashes. Will you take me there?"

"Yes," Captain Petran said without hesitation.

"Why do you think they didn't want to talk about the village?"

"Superstition," he said dismissively. "I had some of these

mountain peasants under my command during the war. Always looking for signs. Omens. I had to constantly bully them to keep them in line."

"Do you think my grandfather was a superstitious peasant?" Josephine asked, feeling the need to defend her relatives.

He smiled. "I don't know what your grandfather was fighting. However, I can't believe it was a monster."

Josephine found Grace cooking dinner with the innkeeper's wife.

"I just wanted to do something familiar. I helped her make dinner: soup with meatballs. I showed her how to make cornbread." Grace smiled and the innkeeper's wife, an older woman, smiled and nodded, though Josephine was pretty sure she didn't understand a word of English. Josephine admired Grace's ability to adapt to an environment that was completely new. *She's discovered a language they have in common—cooking*, Josephine thought, wondering if she could be as clever.

"You can come out with us tomorrow or stay here again," Josephine told Grace as they got ready for bed.

"I'm just fine right here." After a moment, she added, "Unless you need me. I don't mind comin' ifin' you need me."

"No, I'll be fine. The captain is going to go with me," Josephine replied as she took her grandfather's ashes out of her suitcase and set them on a chair.

CHAPTER FIVE

A storm blew through during the night. The wind and thunder caused both women to sleep poorly until the front finally passed in the early hours. When Josephine got out of bed, she could already feel that the weather was cooler.

She was carrying her grandfather's ashes when she met up with the captain, who'd eaten early and had already secured two horses for them.

"Nice looking," Josephine said, walking up to the bay gelding that Captain Petran was leading.

"You sound surprised. We have good horses here. If I may?" he said, taking the jar with the ashes and placing it in one of the saddlebags on his horse.

Both horses were fitted out with old military saddles. Having been warned, Josephine was wearing an old pair of trousers that she'd brought with her, knowing she'd be traversing some rough country.

They rode back to the farm and had an early lunch with her relatives. Most of the men had come in from the fields to eat with her. She gathered that this was quite unusual. Normally, the women would have taken lunch out to where the men were working, but in honor of the strange cousin from America, they had come in to eat.

"Tell them I'm going to the village today," Josephine told the captain.

"I don't think that would be wise," Petran counseled.

"Maybe not. But I want them to know I'm not scared of whatever happened there. Maybe one of them will be brave enough to tell me the truth."

The captain looked hard into her face and realized that she wasn't going to change her mind. He spoke in Romanian to the men and women gathered around the table. Everyone had been smiling, eating and drinking, but as the captain spoke, the smiles dropped away one by one.

Constantin spoke to the captain in rapid, gruff Romanian. Petran answered with a calm but firm voice. Then Constantin said something that made the captain's face flush, and the next words that came from him were delivered in hard, harsh tones.

"What's going on?" Josephine asked, reaching out and grabbing the captain's arm.

"These ignorant peasants warned us not to go near the village. Warned *me*!"

"Tell them that we understand their concern, but I must go to the village out of respect for my grandfather," Josephine said forcefully. She was afraid the captain might let his anger get out of control

But her words had the desired calming effect on him. Looking at her, he nodded and spoke to the gathering. His tone was slow and measured. They listened. Constantin started to speak, but Elena reached out with her gnarled hands and touched his sleeve, addressing him earnestly.

"What's she saying?" Josephine asked.

"She told him that you were right to respect your grandfather's wishes. As with all things, it is in God's hands."

An hour later they left the farm, followed by smiles and well wishes, with only a few disapproving looks from some of the older men.

They had ridden for about ten minutes when the captain stopped at a spot before the path entered a wooded area. He dismounted his horse and reached into his saddlebag.

"I don't like taking chances," he said, pulling out a holster and placing it on his belt. From the holster, he removed a Webley revolver and made sure it was loaded before putting it back into the holster and remounting his horse.

"You don't think somebody would attack us?"

"Peasants," he said as though any illogical behavior was explained by that one word. "Besides, there are bandits in these mountains."

A few minutes later, they were crossing a stream when a horse and rider came crashing down a narrow animal trail toward them. The captain reached for his pistol, but stayed his hand when he realized that it was only Josephine's young cousin, Gheorghe.

"What are you doing here?" the captain asked in Romanian.

"I have something for my cousin. You may need it if you're going to the old village." Gheorghe reached behind himself and unstrapped a leather case about the size and shape of a large loaf of bread. "Here," he said, holding it out.

Josephine sat on her horse, not understanding what they were saying but with a sense of its importance.

The captain nudged his horse forward until he could take the rolled leather kit.

"This was her grandfather's. He left it with the family when he fled to America," the young man said.

"Why did they not give it to her?"

"They're scared. They worry that something might cause the nightmare to come again. I am not afraid." The captain recognized the bravery of youth that had not been tested in the heat of battle.

"Brave, are you? What is this monster your family is so afraid of?"

"I don't know. The troubles were over long before the war."

"You would have thought that the war would have given them other things to fear rather than silly superstitions."

"My family may be scared, but I know they are not cowards. If they fear something, then it is real and dangerous."

"So you say."

The captain unrolled the leather case. Inside were several odd items: a vial of water, a small prayer book, several feet of crudely made rope, a small knife and a bone saw. The captain turned to Josephine and gave her a quick summary of the conversation. Turning back to the young man, he asked, "What is all of this?"

"A hunter's kit. According to my grandfather, the village hired a hunter to kill the beast that was stalking them. He came with this and his guns. Her grandfather and his brothers went with him in search of the creature. Only her grandfather came back. Less than a year later, everyone still alive moved from the village."

"What good is this against a wolf or a bear? Better if you'd brought guns," Petran ridiculed the kit.

"Our people thought the monster was a supernatural being."

"And that's how peasants think." The captain was getting angry again.

"We are not ignorant. My people know more about these hills than any man alive. It's no shame that we couldn't defeat something not of this earth."

The captain shrugged and gave the package to Josephine.

"Thank him for me."

"She thanks you. Now we'll be off," he said to Gheorghe.

"I'm going with you," the youth stated loudly.

Petran looked him up and down appraisingly. "You need to tend your fields."

"You need someone with you who knows the land. Did you know that there is a pass that's not on the maps?"

As the whole reason Petran was in the area was to map it for an improved road system, he had to consider this news carefully. "You know of a pass that's not marked?"

"Yes. It is above the village. My grandfather has told me

about it many times."

"How far from the village?"

"Not far. I can take you there."

"Even though you've never been there?"

"Yes. I've heard the stories many times."

"Very well," Petran told him and then explained the situation to Josephine.

The three of them rode off toward the old village as the day turned into afternoon. The path became more of a deer trail as they approached the settlement. They passed the first abandoned house within an hour. Soon, they were standing in a small area of stone houses with thatched roofs that had fallen in long ago. They dismounted and tied their horses to trees. Josephine walked around, trying to imagine the place filled with families and animals.

She came across a small building where the roof had been made of wood. Looking up, she could see the remains of a small steeple. Behind the old church, she found a collection of gravestones and crosses surrounded by a low stone wall.

Going back to the horses, she retrieved her grandfather's ashes. The captain came over to her.

"I've found a place to scatter his ashes," she said. "The old cemetery. He'll be at rest with his family."

Gheorghe followed them back to the churchyard. Josephine said a prayer as the two men bowed their heads, hats in hand. She spread the ashes over the area while a cool, gentle breeze helped to send them drifting into the far reaches of the graveyard.

Some of the gravestones could still be read. Josephine and Gheorghe walked through them, seeing names that were familiar from their grandparents' stories.

"We'd better go," Petran said, "if we're going to get back to town before nightfall."

"The pass is over there," Gheorghe said, pointing at two small mountain peaks that loomed over the village. The three mounted up and followed a path that had once been a road, but was now little more than an animal trail.

As they approached the pass, a large stone structure came into view between the peaks. A medieval fortress had been built from the stony outcroppings, spanning the gap above the pass. Anyone traveling this way would have had to pass beneath the fortress. Constructed from the same stone as the mountains, the building was nearly impossible to see from a distance. Captain Petran began to understand how it had remained hidden all these years.

"Did you know about this?" Petran asked Gheorghe.

"The old men talked about it in hushed whispers, but I didn't believe them. They said that it had protected them for centuries."

As they entered the pass, Josephine gasped. "There," she said, pointing. "I saw someone."

The captain and Gheorghe looked, but there was no one there. Then suddenly a man appeared in the middle of the road under the fortress.

"Stop!" he yelled loudly in Romanian. The man was large, taller than either the captain or Gheorghe, with broad shoulders. He held a pike in his hands.

"I'm Captain Petran of the Romanian Army!"

"Ha!" was all the man said. He twirled the huge pike threateningly. "I am Balan Lupu, captain of the guard for Baron Dragomir Blasko, once *voivode* of all that you can see from this fortress."

"What is he saying?" Josephine asked in a hushed whisper.

"He is called the Blonde Wolf, and he's the captain of the guard for some baron who was once the governor of this land," Petran explained. Then he turned to Gheorghe and asked in Romanian, "Have you ever heard of this Baron Blasko?"

The young man shook his head.

"Leave here and never return!" Lupu bellowed.

Now that she was able to see the man clearly, he looked older than she'd first thought. His hair was long and grey, his face leathery and lined as though he'd spent decades watching for trespassers.

"I have the authority of the government to survey all lands in these mountains," the captain said.

The big man seemed to have had enough and began to approach them, his large, sturdy pike held at the ready.

"You've been warned. I give you one more chance. Turn and go," Lupu said.

"We should leave," Josephine said, not understanding the words but receiving the message just the same.

The captain said nothing, but drew his service revolver. As the gun cleared his holster, Lupu ran at him, pike extended. The captain fired two quick shots. The first one hit Lupu, who didn't seem to notice, while the second round went high as Lupu closed the distance. Before Petran could react, Lupu thrust the pike into his chest and lifted him off of his horse. When the captain hit the ground, Josephine could hear the sound of the pike ripping through his ribcage.

Somehow Petran managed to steady the gun as he fired another shot into Lupu's chest. The big man staggered, trying to wrestle the pike from the dying captain's body.

Josephine's horse had had enough, spooking at the sight of the maddened, pike-wielding Romanian. She lost control of the reins as the horse reared. Still holding onto the leather kit that Gheorghe had given her, she kicked free of the stirrups and fell to the ground as the horse bolted away. She rolled over to see Lupu, bleeding from his chest and standing over the captain.

Gheorghe had been watching the events unfold from a safe distance, sitting on his horse with his mouth hanging open and his heart hammering in his chest. His mind was a blur of thoughts and emotions that finally crystalized into one goal—saving himself. He turned his horse and galloped back the way they'd come.

As Josephine watched, Lupu twisted the pike, trying to free it. His movements slowed, his knees finally buckling as the blood pumped from the wound in his heart. He slumped to the ground and fell over beside the captain's body.

Horrified, Josephine stumbled to her feet and stared at the bodies on the ground. The captain's horse had also run off, leaving her the only living thing standing in the road in front of the medieval fortress.

What the hell do I do now? her inner voice screamed.

She looked down at the kit in her hand. *Not much protection here*, she thought, trying to think of a plan that would end with her safe and sound back at the inn. Or, better yet, back home in Alabama.

Looking again at Petran and Lupu, she noticed the Webley revolver lying on the ground near the captain's outstretched arm. She carefully walked around the bodies and picked it up. Petran had shot three times, so there should be three rounds left—assuming that he wasn't like her father, who had always kept an empty cylinder under the hammer.

Josephine had to work a little to figure out how to open up the gun. It was a top break, unlike the Colt revolvers she was used to. As she'd suspected, there were three rounds left. *Do I have the nerve to search his pockets?* she asked herself. Josephine shut her eyes for just a second, then thought, *If I'm going to survive, then I have to do whatever is necessary. No time for niceties.*

She quickly kneeled down before she lost her nerve. Petran's body was still warm as she went through his pockets. She found a lighter, a cigarette case, his papers and nothing else. She kept the lighter and an official-looking letter that had his name on it. She kept the paper so that if she ever got out of there, she'd be able to let someone know what had happened to him.

The sun was falling behind the mountains and the temperature was dropping fast. Josephine would have taken the captain's coat, but it was a bloody mess. She shivered.

It would take her most of a day to walk back to her relatives' farm, and at night it would be impossible. The paths were too poorly marked and there would be only a sliver of a moon. Attempting to walk back now would only result in her getting lost and dying in the wilderness. *And when I do get back to the farm, I will spit in Gheorghe's face*, she vowed.

A wolf howled in the distance and another answered. Pushing away the grim thought of being eaten, Josephine turned around and looked at the fortress looming over the pass. *I don't have much choice*, she told herself. *Surely, if there are other killer giants inside, they would have come out by now.*

Josephine squared her shoulders and walked toward the castle, holding the revolver and her grandfather's kit tightly. The door that Lupu had obviously come out of was still ajar. She opened it and walked through into the darkness, taking out the captain's lighter and flicking it on. The flame illuminated a well-worn stone staircase that spiraled up out of sight.

After she had climbed about twenty steps, natural light began to seep through from above. Josephine continued up until she came to what appeared to be a large, ancient banquet hall. There were several massive wooden tables and a fireplace that half a dozen men could have stood in with ease.

What do I do now? she wondered. *Continue searching the castle, or hunker down here for the night and leave first thing in the morning?*

There was some wood by the fireplace and that made up her mind. With a fire, she would be able to last the night. There was no reason to risk disturbing anyone… or anything… living within the bowels of the fortress.

CHAPTER SIX

Josephine was soon comforted by the warm flames glowing brightly in the fireplace. Outside, the light coming in through the ancient rippled glass of the great hall had faded to a dull blue. She walked through the large room quickly and checked all the doors. They couldn't be locked, but with some effort she was able to slide two heavy wooden chairs in front of them. If anyone tried to enter the room, at least she'd have some warning.

She placed the revolver on the floor beside her and, using the rolled leather kit as a crude pillow, curled up beside the hearth in the soothing light of the flames. Darkness fell as she tended the fire and tried to rest.

Much later, she was startled awake when a voice spoke to her from several feet away.

"*Cine esti?*"

Josephine could see a large figure, barely lit by the dim light of the dying fire. "I don't understand," she said, sitting up and reaching for the revolver. The gun was gone.

"You speak English?" the man asked with a heavy accent. His face was still hidden in shadows.

"Yes."

"Did you come with the man who killed Lupu?" The

voice held only a hint of accusation.

"Yes," Josephine repeated, not seeing the point in lying.

"Why have you come here?"

"I came…" She didn't know if he meant to Romania or just to this castle. "My grandfather was born in the village below."

"And that gives you the right to come here and kill my servant?"

"No, of course not. But he attacked us!" She couldn't help but defend herself and Captain Petran.

"Lupu's job was to protect my home and the pass it is built upon."

Feeling vulnerable on the floor, Josephine scrambled to her feet, causing the leather-bound kit that she'd been using as a pillow to roll toward the stranger. The man flew forward so fast that her eyes could barely follow him in the dim light. He snatched up the leather satchel and unrolled it. Seeing the implements inside, he dropped it to the floor with an exclamation of disgust.

Josephine could see the man clearly now. While he wasn't very tall, his wide shoulders and broad chest made him appear larger than he actually was. His hair was black with a hint of grey at the temples. Thin, dark eyebrows hovered above large green eyes. His cheek bones were high and provided the perfect frame for his sloping nose. He was dressed in an Edwardian suit that looked worn with age.

He stared at her and his eyes burned red like the fanned coals of a fire. He raised his hands and stretched his long, elegant fingers toward her. "You came here to kill me," he snarled.

"I did not!" she exclaimed, backing away from him.

"Liar! You bring a gun and these… tools to destroy me and still you try and deny it?" He was advancing toward her with each word.

Josephine had no more words to defend herself from someone who was obviously mad. Escape was her only option. She looked around the room, but the darkness prevented her from seeing any avenues of hope. As she backed away from him, she bumped into one of the huge wooden tables and ducked underneath it. Coming up on the other side, she felt a little better having the solid object between them. But as she continued backing toward the far wall, the man approached the table and shoved it out of his way as if it weighed nothing.

Shaking now, Josephine knew she was trapped and in mortal danger. One thought ran through her head, helping to rally her. *I will fight. To my last breath, I will fight.*

The man lunged toward her, grabbing her shoulder. With irresistible strength he pulled her toward him and savagely bit into her neck. She managed to jerk her head aside at the last moment, preventing him from tearing into a vital artery. But still he drew blood.

Fight fire with fire, she thought, biting down on the hand still holding onto her shoulder. She clamped her jaws with a force she didn't think possible and blood from his hand filled her mouth. She choked, drinking in some of the fluid against her will.

As soon as she swallowed, a strange feeling came over her. It was a calmness that seemed completely out of place in the horror scene that was playing out in the great hall. At the same time, the man gave an ear-piercing scream and cast her away from him.

For a moment, she thought that the bite had caused this reaction, but he didn't seem to care about his hand. His eyes were focused on her with hatred and something new... dread.

"What have you done?" he screamed at her. "Stupid woman!"

Josephine was taken aback. "You attacked me, you bastard! Surely you didn't think I wouldn't defend myself." Adrenaline was pulsing through her veins. She could see flecks of her blood glistening on his lips, but she didn't feel any pain.

"You drank my blood!" His voice was cold fury.

"You were trying to chew my damn neck off!" she yelled back, still stunned at the sudden change of events.

"I was only going to kill you!"

"Exactly!"

"Bah! You are ignorant. What you've done is a thousand times worse," he said bitterly.

"You must be the baron that Lupu was talking about." Josephine was finally gaining enough composure to begin thinking rationally.

"Don't pretend you didn't know who I was. You came here to kill me."

"I did not! I don't even know why you think that. Clearly you're mad."

"Of course I'm mad, you idiot. You bit me and drank my blood."

"Not mad as in angry. Mad as in crazy as a bat out of hell."

"You are the crazy one. Coming into my castle, planning on attacking me in my bed."

Josephine threw up her hands in frustration. "I was *not* planning to kill you! Your ogre attacked and killed my friend, leaving me alone out there. I came in here to keep from dying of the cold. My plan, my *only* plan, was to wait until morning and then get as far away from this gothic lair of yours as possible." She felt her neck. Her shirt was damp with blood and the pain was beginning to register. "I can't believe you bit me, you... ass."

"You drank my blood," he repeated morosely. He took off his coat and ripped a strip off of his shirtsleeve, handing it to her. "Here. Stop the bleeding."

Josephine took the fabric reluctantly and held it to her neck. She couldn't understand why he was so upset. "Yeah, well, that'll teach you to go around attacking women. You didn't even ask me my name first," she said irrationally.

"I'm supposed to introduce myself to someone who's broken into my castle with the intent to decapitate me?"

"What the hell are you talking about? How could I

possibly decapitate you?" For Josephine, the conversation was devolving into nonsense.

"Of course, you didn't plan on your soldier being killed. No doubt he was the one who was going to saw my head off with that instrument." The man pointed toward the leather kit. It had spilled open when he dropped it on the floor and the bone saw within caught the reflection of the last light from the fireplace.

Josephine sighed. "I *told* you. My grandfather lived in the village before he immigrated to America. I came back here to scatter his ashes. One of my relatives gave me that. I had no plans to use it for anything."

"Who are you?"

"Now you ask? My name is Josephine Nicolson."

"Nicolson? That wasn't your grandfather's name."

"It was Americanized. His Romanian name was Nicolescu."

"Yes, they lived in the village. I remember them."

Remember them? Josephine thought. *He is insane.* Aloud she said, "He left here almost seventy years ago."

"That long," he muttered.

"Sorry, but I don't remember what your buddy with the pike said your name was," Josephine said, casting her eyes around for an easy exit. Could she outrun him?

The man looked at her, his eyes now cool and thoughtful. "I'm Baron Dragomir Blasko," he finally said, seemingly unable to prevent himself from giving her a slight bow.

Even with her mind racing to find a way out of this nightmare, a revelation came to her. "Wait. You're the monster my grandfather was hunting?"

Blasko waved his hand. "That is a story for another day. Currently, we have another problem. One that you caused."

"Me?"

"I was just going to rip out your throat. You would have been dead in mere seconds. But now..." He shook his head grimly and dropped dramatically into a chair.

"Excuse me, but I actually prefer not to be dead."

"That is because you are ignorant," he said in a snarky tone.

"So help me, if you call me ignorant one more time..." Josephine felt her hand curl into a fist.

"You'll what? Kill me? You can't kill me now."

"I'm supposed to just wait until you fly into another murderous rage and come after me again?"

"I can't kill you either."

"Why not? You were certainly willing to do it ten minutes ago!" Josephine was frustrated and rapidly losing her fear of the man. Despite what she'd said about her grandfather, she wasn't really buying the monster thing. Blasko was just an insane hermit. Albeit a well-dressed insane hermit.

"We are now kin."

"What the hell are you talking about?"

"Blood of my blood," Blasko muttered, putting his head in his hands.

Josephine didn't know what he was talking about, but she was determined to take advantage of his apparent depression to escape. If she had to kill him in the process, then she would. She sidled over toward the leather kit. "I still don't understand," she said as she moved, trying to keep him talking.

"Arrggh!" he moaned in frustration. "We drank each other's blood. We are now kin. I can't kill you and you can't kill me. We are inseparable. Is that plain enough for you?" He was staring down at the floor.

"No kidding?" she asked, going along with his ravings and hoping that he wouldn't get worked up again.

"Yes." He looked up at her. "Hah! I see you creeping toward your vampire hunter's kit. Be my guest. Try and kill me."

"Don't make me do it."

"Are you stupid? Didn't you hear what I just said?" He stood up and came toward her.

"Stay back!"

She grabbed for the kit and tore through it, pulling out

the sharp silver dagger. She held it out in front of her, pointing it at Blasko, who kept coming closer. "Stop!" she yelled, jabbing with the knife in his direction. He kept coming. "I'm not fooling around."

Blasko stopped a foot in front of her.

"Stab me. Go ahead. Try and kill me."

"I... I'm not angry enough," Josephine said lamely.

Blasko opened his mouth and hissed at her, revealing sharpened fangs, and his eyes burned red again. He was only inches from her face. Reacting on impulse, Josephine tried to stab him, but nothing happened. Her arm refused to thrust the knife forward, no matter how hard she tried. Scared now, Josephine could only stare at him as the knife fell to the floor.

Blasko closed his mouth and his eyes returned to their cool green stare. "I'll say it one more time. We cannot kill each other. If one of us dies, the other will become inconsolable... hopeless."

"You're lying."

"Listen, woman—"

Josephine held up her hand, frustration battling with her fear. "Stop it right there. My name is Josephine Nicolson."

Blasko huffed. "I was only going to say that you need to start listening to me. I'm trying to educate you. To tell you what a mess you've caused."

"We're going over the same ground. You attacked me. If you hadn't done that, then I wouldn't have bitten you. The blame lies with you." Josephine was letting her anger lead her now. What was there to lose?

"Wo... Miss Nicolson. We have established that you entered my castle without permission and with the intent of killing me. I defended myself. The blame is yours."

"I told you, I did *not* come here to kill you."

"But you brought that." He pointed to the kit on the floor.

"I explained about that!"

"Enough! We must both accept that what is done is

done. Now we must come to terms."

"What do you mean 'terms'?"

"We must decide how to proceed."

"That might be easier if you explained who... or *what* you are," Josephine said through clenched teeth.

"I don't need... Fine. Maybe you have a point." Blasko sighed and sat back down. "The Muslims called me a *giaour*. My own people call me a *vampir*. I need blood to live."

Josephine stared at him in horror. "You *are* a monster," she exclaimed after a speechless moment.

"I don't have to defend myself to you."

"You do. You *do* have..." Josephine stopped, realizing he was right that it was too late to play the blame game. "And now you've infected me."

Blasko shook his head. "You are not like me. For that to happen, there is much more to the... transition ceremony. Only once have I ever created another, and I won't do it again. Besides, you can only be turned willingly. You would have to want the change with all your heart."

"But then why—"

"Having shared each others' blood, we are forever connected. Our souls are locked together. The blood of the *vampir* has tremendous power."

"Great," Josephine said sarcastically. "I'll just leave then, shall I?"

"No, that won't be possible."

"What do you mean, that's not possible? If you can't kill me, and I can't kill you, then what's the point in me hanging around?"

"The connection between us is too strong. Neither of us would survive a separation of significant distance."

"Excuse me, but as we say in Alabama, that's bullshit! I'm going home!"

"Try if you want." Blasko shrugged. "But you will fall into a deep melancholy that will consume you."

"I'll take my chances," Josephine said bravely, but even as she said the words she felt an odd tugging at her emotions.

This is crazy! she thought, walking toward the door. But in her heart she feared he was telling the truth. She felt her legs giving out and she quickly found a chair, dropping into it.

Blasko stared at her knowingly. After a moment, he said, "The effect is most intense right after infection. It will ease a bit with time…" He stood and walked toward the door. "I'll give you a while to think. I need to go clean up your mess."

Josephine sat there, pondering her fate. Staying in the castle was not an option. But what other choice did she have? Slowly, a wild idea formed in her mind.

CHAPTER SEVEN

Two hours later, the baron was back. "I took the captain's body down to the path between the old village and the new. Most of the peasants are too scared to venture any farther," he told her.

Josephine wondered if she should tell him about the young man that had been with them, but she decided not to. "And your friend?"

"I buried him," Blasko said with no emotion.

While Josephine had seen his display of strength, it still seemed incredible he could have moved the captain's body and buried Lupu in only a couple of hours.

"How did you learn English?"

"Over many years. I've known a few Englishmen, and lately I've listened to the radio."

"You have a radio?" It seemed an odd thing to have in this medieval castle.

"I'm not a primitive."

"How old are you?" Josephine asked, not sure if she was prepared to believe his answer.

"Hundreds of years. But now is not the time to discuss my history."

"I'm leaving. I've made up my mind," she threw at him.

"I thought I explained—"

"Perfectly," she interrupted. "We can't be separated by thousands of miles. That's why you are coming with me."

"Ha! You are a fool! You know nothing about how I'm forced to live. I can't possibly travel to another continent."

"I'm sure we can get around any difficulties. No doubt I'll have to help you. You probably can't understand our modern ways."

She watched him as he puffed himself up. "Bah! I understand everything. I'm ancient, not ignorant. I have money. I've traveled through Europe. You have nothing to teach me!"

"Fine, then it shouldn't be a problem," Josephine said lightly.

"I must sleep during the day. I need nourishment. It is very... difficult for me to cross running water." He said this last as though he was embarrassed by the weakness.

"Maybe a box of some sort might be in order."

"Well... Yes. I've used a box to travel in the past. To avoid the direct rays of the sun and the... river problem."

"You can live in my house in Alabama until we get this all figured out. There's a priest in town that might be able to help us."

The baron hissed. "No priest. Ever."

Josephine ignored him. "How long can you go without food or water?"

"I presume you mean comfortably? But this does not matter. I'm not going to Alabama." He sounded like a petulant child refusing to go to bed.

"You're the one who said we can't be separated," she reminded him. "And I'm not staying here."

Blasko began to pace. Josephine kept quiet, sitting back in her chair and letting him work it out.

"I need to feed at least once a week. Human blood."

Josephine felt a cold shiver go up her spine. "I can't bring people to you to feast on," she said, horrified.

"I don't need people. I need their blood. I've stayed alive

these last hundred years without taking innocent lives," he said haughtily.

Innocent lives? Does that mean he's taken the lives of people he didn't consider innocent? Josephine wondered. "How...?"

"Don't you listen? I told you I have men who are loyal to me. They are willing to bleed themselves for me. In return, I have kept the land surrounding the fortress as a safe haven for them."

"Criminals?"

"Ahh... Some of them are descendants of men who have fought with me for centuries. Others deserted the army during the Great War. They survive as... bandits. I keep them from preying on the villagers. They only rob from strangers who grow fat off of others."

Josephine was dubious of this Robin Hood honor system, but now didn't seem the time to debate it. "So if you were given blood like doctors use for transfusions, then...?"

"Yes, that would be acceptable. I would be able to see the New World. I will admit that the thought... intrigues me," he said thoughtfully.

"I want to make this clear. Killing people is not acceptable in America," Josephine told him.

He burst out laughing. "I told you I have a radio. I know what it's like in Chicago. I know about that man Capone and the one they call Baby Face. Killing people is a pastime in your country," Blasko said with more levity than any time since she'd met him. She started to protest, but he shook his head vigorously. "I know, I know. I will not kill your countrymen. I'll let them kill themselves."

"How do you contact your... friends? We'll need their help."

"Come with me," he said, walking quickly toward one of the doors.

"By the way, where is the captain's gun? I had it with me before you discovered me," Josephine said to his back.

Blasko whirled around and pulled the gun from his jacket, then held it out to her. "Take it."

Gun in hand, she followed him to a circular stairway. Up and around they went, until Josephine thought her legs would give out. Finally, they reached the top and came out onto a large turret that was maybe thirty feet across. She looked over the battlements. The ground was far below in the darkness. In the center of the turret was a stone fire pit with wood stacked, waiting for a match to light it afire.

"Damn, I forgot a torch. I'll have to go—"

Josephine stopped him by pulling Petran's lighter from her pocket.

"Ahhh, thank you." Blasko used the lighter and soon there were flames rising six feet in the air. The wind was gusting, sending sparks high to mingle with the stars. "We'll have to wait. It may be tomorrow afternoon, but someone will come."

Josephine looked out over the mountains. The turret was even with the two peaks that formed the pass, but to the south and north she could see for twenty-five miles or more. She felt wild and free standing on the ancient stone battlements.

It's odd, she thought. *Here I am chained to this strange creature and yet I feel free and alive. What must Grace be thinking? Did Gheorghe go back and tell everyone what happened?* She sighed. *Do I always have to be worried about tomorrow?*

Josephine looked over at Blasko, who was staring out over the mountains with an odd expression on his face. The fire at his back cast his shadow on the stone walls. *What must he be thinking?* she wondered. *Saying goodbye to his homeland?*

Blasko looked out over the valleys and mountains only dimly lit by the stars. His thoughts would have surprised Josephine. *Good riddance, you ignorant peasants. How many years have I fought to protect you and received only hatred and loathing in return? We'll see how you fare without Baron Dragomir Blasko to protect the passes.*

They stood there together for an hour until the horizon began to turn pale blue. "I must go in now," Blasko said. Josephine followed him back down to the great hall.

"Luca Petrescu should be here today. He has moved me before. He'll know what needs to be done."

Blasko sat down at a large wooden table against the wall. He took a pen and paper and wrote out some instructions, using his signet ring to seal it with wax.

"Now there will be no question that these are my orders," Blasko said, handing her the letter. "Also, he will tell you what my needs will be during the trip. Do not fail to follow his instructions to the letter." He stood up. "You will excuse me now." There was a hint of anxiety in his voice as the light from the window continued to brighten.

Josephine watched him leave, a strange melancholy falling upon her. *Is this part of the... curse?* she wondered. *Or is it simply weariness from the longest and strangest night of my life?*

Luca didn't arrive at the fortress until noon. He was short and wiry, wearing knee-high boots and riding a large black horse. Except for his height, he was the very model of a highwayman. He assessed the situation rapidly after reading Blasko's note and Josephine was relieved to find out that he spoke some English.

"I take you to woods. You pretend. They think you wander away from castle. Pretend, yes?" He made a face like a crazy person. "They think you not right. The fright, it make you no remember."

Josephine understood and told him so.

"First, I show you baron. Follow, please?" he instructed, walking backward toward the castle.

She followed him down into the depths of the structure. In a room far below ground level was a crypt. Inside, on an ancient marble pedestal, was a centuries-old coffin made out of a beautiful ebony wood. There were no markings on the box. Its shape and the four silver handles were the only clues that it was a coffin.

Josephine frowned as Luca went into great detail regarding the proper care and feeding of the baron. She thought some of the details were more convention than necessity, but she would follow them to the letter.

Luca told her which train the baron would be on and made her swear she would be on that train too. Josephine was amazed at the bandit's knowledge of the local train timetables. *I guess it goes with the job*, she thought cynically.

Climbing up on the saddle behind him, Josephine was whisked back down the trail and through the woods past the old village to an area out of sight, but not too far, from her relatives' farm. After watching Luca ride away, Josephine got down in the dirt and rolled around, making herself look dirty and unkempt. With the final addition of a few sticks in her hair, she got up and trotted toward the farm.

Josephine ran into some of her relatives in the first field she passed. From their expressions, it was clear that they'd had no idea she was anywhere nearby. Apparently, Gheorghe hadn't bothered to mention the "incident" at the pass the day before. At first it irritated Josephine, but she figured out pretty fast that it could work to her advantage. It was also useful that no one spoke English beyond a few words.

Soon, she was being carried to town in the back of a wagon. Grace came running out to meet her before Josephine's feet even touched the ground. They exchanged hugs.

"I was about to rustle up some proper police to come lookin' for you," Grace said, a huge smile on her face.

"I'm so glad to see you," Josephine said, squeezing Grace's hand.

"Whoooeee, what happened to your neck? Come on in here and let me clean that up."

Grace led Josephine inside the inn. Through hand signals and a few words with the innkeeper, she managed to get some soap, water and linen to clean and bandage Josephine's wound.

"We need to pack. We're leaving first thing in the morning."

"Praise the Lord, that's the best news I've heard in a

while. You liked to scare me to death being gone like that."

By sun-up, they were on their way back to Curtea de Arges to meet the train. Josephine had no idea how she was going to explain their extra baggage to Grace. The truth seemed too risky. *But do I have a choice?* Josephine thought.

As they bumped their way down the road toward the train station, Josephine could feel a strange tugging at her heart, like a compass needle searching for the North Pole. Was something inside of her searching for Blasko? The idea was ridiculous, yet she wondered...

"I have to tell you something you probably won't understand," Josephine started. Grace looked at her expectantly, but suddenly Josephine decided to take a different tack. "How would you like to make more money?" she blurted.

Grace stared at her, trying to decide if she'd heard what she thought she'd heard. "I'd like that a whole bunch," she finally said, thinking Josephine must have hit her head while she was lost in the woods. But then again, white folk were strange. She knew she'd have to be careful. Grace had heard stories and most of the ones that started out with a white person being kind to a black person didn't end well for the black person.

"I can give you a sizable raise, but I'm going to need something from you in return."

Uh oh, Grace thought, *here it comes*. Aloud she said, "I got to know what it is 'for I can say yes or no."

"All you need to do is be quiet about... something. Really quiet. Not like only-telling-some-people quiet. But never-tell-*anyone* quiet," Josephine said.

Grace chewed on this as the carriage rocked along the road. *I want to know how much money*, she thought. *But I don't want to make her mad. Wish I knew what the big secret was. With white folk, there's no telling.* That's when it became obvious to Grace what the secret had to be. Miss Josephine must be pregnant. *Boring*, she thought. *The daddy is probably that big lunk Bobby Tucker. That would explain why he was hanging around the house so much before we left.*

The more time Grace took to answer, the more nervous Josephine became. She knew that Grace was pretty religious, so she was probably having a hard time agreeing to keeping a secret. No doubt she was afraid that it was something immoral. She couldn't take Grace's silence anymore and decided to make an offer that was beyond generous. "I'll pay you thirty-five dollars a week."

Grace almost fainted. *She must be pregnant with twins*, was the first thought that popped into her head. With that kind of salary, Grace could take care of both herself and her brother's family.

"I'll do it!" Grace couldn't imagine any secret she wouldn't be willing to keep for that amount of money.

Josephine had seen her father make financial deals both with farmers and some of the richest men in the county. Whenever they wanted to seal the pact in an ironclad fashion, there was only one way for it to be done. Josephine turned up her hand and, locking eyes with Grace, she spat into her hand and held it out.

Grace looked at Josephine and knew she was making a deal with the devil for sure. No white man or woman would ever spit in their hand and then shake with a black person. Not unless they were agreeing to something terrible. *I should say no*, a little voice in her head said. *You need that money, fool!* shouted her more practical side. Before she could change her mind, Grace spat into her hand and shook with Josephine.

The box containing the baron was waiting at the station when they reached Curtea de Arges. According to Luca, Blasko wouldn't need to feed until they reached Cherbourg. Along with the coffin, he had sent a few other boxes, including one with bottles of blood packed in ice. Luckily the weather was still cool, but even so the ice would be melted by the time they reached France. Josephine would have to feed Blasko and repack the blood to keep it cool for the trip across the Atlantic.

Josephine felt better just being on the train with Blasko. *An insane reaction considering what a pain in the ass this is going to be*, she thought.

Josephine had decided not to reveal the truth to Grace until they were back in Alabama. She had been curious about the boxes, but she wasn't pressing Josephine for answers. Wisely, Grace had decided that not asking questions was one of her new duties.

Surprisingly, everything went smoothly during the trip and, in less than two weeks' time, they were pulling up in front of Josephine's house, followed by a truck bearing their luggage and three large crates.

CHAPTER EIGHT

Present...

Josephine didn't believe Blasko had killed Samuel Erickson, but she couldn't deny that this was a disturbing development.

"I told you he was going to kill somebody. Didn't I?" Grace insisted, following Josephine down the stairs.

"I heard you the first dozen times. The baron didn't kill him. I'm... sure of it."

"I don't know how you can be sure. Him up walkin' around all night while the rest of us are sleepin'."

"You know he's allergic to the sun. He only has the nighttime," Josephine said, turning to face Grace. She wanted to go down to the basement and talk with Blasko, but she knew that if Grace followed her it would just turn into a giant pig-wrestling match of a mess. "I'll deal with this. You need to get back to work."

Grace stared at her. She'd kept Josephine's secret for almost six months, but it was wearing on her nerves. A naturally garrulous person, she was finding it hard to spend time with her friends and not gossip about the blood-drinking freak in the basement. Everyone knew that Blasko was staying with Josephine, but no one but Josephine and

Grace knew his true nature.

Sometimes Grace wondered if there was more to the story than Josephine had shared with her, but the bottom line was that, in her heart, she'd come to trust Josephine more than any white person she'd ever known. Besides, she needed the extra money Josephine was paying to help her brother and his family.

"Whatever you say, Miss Josephine," Grace said reluctantly, turning to go. "But he's goin' to kill all of us in our beds, sure 'nough," she muttered as she walked away.

Josephine sighed. At least I can talk to him alone for a second. Still wearing her robe, she knocked on the door under the stairs that led to the basement. Most homes in southern Alabama didn't have basements, but Josephine's neighborhood was built on one of the highest hills in the county. On the hill, more than a dozen houses touted cellars. The Nicolsons had used it mostly for storage until Josephine had brought Blasko home. He'd spent the last several months remodeling it.

Blasko opened the door, dressed in an ornate burgundy housecoat that was more suited to the turn of the century. His disdain of modern culture could be cringe-worthy.

Josephine felt something slink past her legs. Poe had decided that Blasko was his soulmate. Every evening the black cat pushed his way into the basement as soon as the door was opened.

"What? You know that I've just risen," Blasko grumbled. He was always at his worst first thing in the evening.

"I need to talk with you," Josephine told him, stepping forward to let him know that this wasn't a conversation for the doorway.

"Very well. Come down," Blasko said reluctantly, turning to walk back down the newly installed walnut staircase that was ornately carved with images of plants and animals native to the Carpathian Mountains.

As she followed him, Josephine thought she heard an odd squeaking sound. It seemed to be coming from the shadows cast by the rafters. Maybe it's the rats Poe hunts. All I know is I never heard squeaking down here before Blasko arrived, she thought.

"A man was killed across the street," Josephine told him once they were standing in his parlor. He was enamored with the Victorian period and the room looked like a cross between a bordello and Queen Victoria's Silver Jubilee barge. He spent his own money, she reminded herself every time she saw it.

"Tragic," Blasko said, sounding bored. "Anyone I've met?" He'd picked up a meerschaum pipe from the mantel and was looking at it closely.

"This is important," Josephine said, exasperated with his attitude.

"I'm sure it is. But I'm not convinced that it's important to me." He set the pipe down and looked at her.

"Would you consider the police searching your rooms important?" Josephine asked.

"They wouldn't dare!" the baron said, realizing at the same time that he had no idea what the constabulary in this country could or couldn't do.

"If Grace is right and Mr. Erickson was murdered, then they're going to be searching every nook and cranny close to the murder scene."

"Surely not in this neighborhood. You told me yourself that even in this country, money has privileges."

"Sadly, if it had been a poor person that was murdered, then no, they probably wouldn't bother us. But Mr. Erickson was the richest man in the county. Not just rich, he was also politically connected. The man was mayor for ten years."

"Ah, I begin to see your point."

"Did you have anything to do with this?

"Bah, why would I kill some stranger?" Blasko said dismissively.

"Well…" Josephine let the obvious implication hang in the air.

Blasko rolled his eyes dramatically. "I get enough…

nourishment thanks to you," he said, sounding aggrieved at the suggestion. But he wasn't being entirely truthful. The current situation was keeping him alive, but he'd felt himself growing weaker over time.

Josephine picked up a hint of hesitation in his voice, but she dismissed it. His need for blood still made her uncomfortable. Once she had figured out how to get blood shipped to the house from a medical supply company in Atlanta, for an exorbitant amount of money, she had allowed herself to hope that it would be the last time she'd have to think about it.

"Besides, if he was just discovered, then he was probably killed this afternoon. How could I possibly have done it? You shouldn't throw around accusations without evidence," Blasko continued.

Josephine knew that his fascination with the Victorian era extended to literature, including the stories of Sherlock Holmes. More than once, he'd tried his deductive powers on the household and visitors with very limited success.

"You have a point. I'll have to find out when he was killed," Josephine said.

"A murder, you say?" Blasko mused, becoming intrigued in spite of himself.

"If it was murder, then they'll probably arrest the person soon," Josephine said, not liking his tone.

"But you could be right. This could pose a threat to me. I should probably look into it. You said the murder occurred across the street?"

"Never mind. I'll go talk to Grace and see if I can get more details," Josephine said, hoping to shut him down.

"I'll be dressed in a minute. I can probably do a better job questioning her."

Damn, Josephine thought. "Dragomir, you know she's not very comfortable around you."

"Impertinent servant. I really don't understand why you haven't fired her," he said dismissively as he walked into the room where he kept his bed—the coffin he'd traveled in from Romania—and a couple wardrobes full of clothes.

"Really, you shouldn't talk to her right now. She's very upset," Josephine insisted.

"You might be right. If she is hysterical, then I'll get more accurate information from the police!" Blasko shouted from his bedroom.

How do I head this off? Josephine's mind was racing. I never should have told him. After six months, she knew that when Blasko got the wind in his sails, there was no way to stop him. The best thing she could do was to find out as much as she could from Grace. Please don't let this really be a murder, she hoped.

Josephine went back upstairs and quickly finished dressing. Then she went hunting for Grace, finding her staring out the front window at the frantic comings and goings across the street.

"What exactly did Myra tell you?" Josephine asked the maid.

"Not much. She couldn't hardly stand, she was so shaken up. Was yellin' to everyone that he was beaten to death. Blood was everywhere, Myra said." Grace paused and looked at Josephine. "You didn't tell him to get out, did you?"

"No. The baron didn't beat Mr. Erickson to death," Josephine said, trying to sound as sure as she could. "Besides, Mr. Erickson would have had to be killed during the day. And you know the baron can't go out in the sunlight."

"Whoever heard of someone who can't go out when the good Lord's sun is shinin'? You know that man's the devil," Grace said, shaking her head.

"That's ridiculous. He's a little... peculiar. But the devil? Not that." A demon, maybe, Josephine couldn't help thinking.

They heard the sound of the basement door opening and closing. Blasko came striding past them, heading for the front door. Josephine had to be quick to catch him before he got outside, wedging herself between the baron and the door.

"Going over there isn't a good idea."

"Of course it is. I might be able to help them with their investigations."

"Sheriff Logan doesn't like people butting in on his job," Josephine said, speaking from personal experience. Two years ago, they'd had a problem with a teller who was stealing from the bank. Every time Josephine had tried to point out something that might have helped the sheriff's investigation, he had almost bitten her head off. At one point, he had told Josephine's father to keep her locked up in the house.

"I'm sure that, as one lawman to another, we'll get along well," Blasko said, trying to maneuver around Josephine.

"You, a lawman! When?"

"As the voivode of the district, I also acted as the magistrate when necessary." Again he tried to get around her, but she continued to block his way.

"How long ago?" she asked, looking over his shoulder to make sure Grace couldn't hear.

"A hundred years or so." He waved his hand dismissively. "But detective work is the same today as then."

"Fingerprints?"

"No, of course there weren't fingerprints. Well, there were fingerprints, but we couldn't collect them. Doesn't matter. People are the same. They kill for the same reasons now that they killed then. With few exceptions, their methods haven't changed. Now, blast it, you were the one who thought we should be worried about this murder. I'm trying to do something to prevent the investigation from spilling over into our house and here you are blocking my way." Blasko was exasperated. He thought Josephine might be the most contrary creature he'd ever met.

"Fine, if you think you can help them, then be my guest." Josephine moved out of his way, bowing sarcastically as she did so.

"That's better," Blasko said, ignoring her tone. Blasko

opened the door, grabbed a hat from the rack by the door and donned it with a flourish, then nodded to her. "I'll return shortly."

"If they don't throw you in jail," Josephine said loudly enough for him to hear her as he walked away.

Blasko strode across the street. Gawkers had already started to gather outside of the Erickson house. Some of the bystanders were holding lanterns of one sort or another and had the look of a mob waiting to jump into action.

The home was a large, square brick edifice with four columns and a narrow, unwelcoming front porch. As Blasko reached the steps leading up to the entrance, Sheriff Tom Logan came barging out of the front door, followed by a deputy.

"We need to get some men down to the depot."

"Men?" Deputy Willard Paige asked. He was one of only three deputies in the county, and not especially quick.

"Deputize some men to help!" Logan shouted at him. "Search the railyard too. Got to be some hobo. Who the devil are you?" This last was directed at Blasko.

"Baron Dragomir Blasko," he answered with a slight bow.

"What the hell are you doing here?" the sheriff asked with narrowed eyes.

"He's staying with me," Josephine responded, coming up the walk as quickly as she could. She'd followed Blasko across the street, knowing that he couldn't be trusted to stay out of trouble.

Logan's eyes shifted back and forth between Blasko and Josephine. The sheriff looked like what he was—a tough, grizzled old lawman. He'd served in the military before the Great War and had gotten a sizable piece of shrapnel in his left thigh that caused him to walk with a slight hitch to his step.

"I don't have time for socializing. We have a murder on

our hands." He wouldn't have bothered adding the last part, but the sheriff was an elected official and even someone as unconcerned with social niceties as Logan recognized the need to explain things to an important citizen such as Josephine Nicolson.

"The murder is the very reason I'm here," Blasko said, causing the sheriff to once again narrow his eyes and stare at him.

"What do you know about it?"

"Nothing yet. But I plan to find out who the murderer is."

"What—" Logan started to say exactly what he was thinking, but then remembered Josephine and that she'd just said this was a guest of hers. He stared back at her.

"He's from Romania," Josephine responded lamely, trying to think of a way to explain Blasko.

"I was a magistrate for my province in Romania. I'm offering you my services in this matter," Blasko said, waving his hand in the general direction of the Erickson house.

"Don't know what the hell you're talking about," Logan said. "We need to get going. The murderer is probably catching a train as we speak."

He started to push past Blasko, who stood his ground. Logan's face turned red and Josephine stepped in quickly.

"Perhaps we could go in and comfort Lucy and the girls," Josephine suggested reasonably. She moved up behind Blasko, unobtrusively taking his arm.

"Sure. Good idea. Doc McGuire is comin' to check over the body," Logan said, moving around Blasko. Deputy Paige, who had stood back and watched the confrontation between Blasko and his boss, tipped his hat to Josephine as they hurried down the walk toward their waiting car.

"You people stay back. Don't go near the house!" the sheriff shouted to the crowd out by the road. It was growing larger as rumor of the murder spread through the small town.

"Come on," Josephine said to Blasko.

They were led into the house by Myra, Grace's friend and the Ericksons' housekeeper. The woman was much larger than Grace and a few years older. She looked overwhelmed by the turn of events.

The house was a standard four and four, with a parlor, study, dining room and bedroom that had been converted into a kitchen downstairs, while the upstairs held four more bedrooms.

Myra escorted them into the parlor where three women and a man were gathered.

"Lucy, how terrible," Josephine said, rushing over to the older woman, who seemed surprised to see her. Josephine understood the look. They were acquaintances because they both were members of the same social circle, but neither would have called the other a friend. Lucy was Samuel Erickson's second wife. His first had died while giving birth to their son, Clarence. *I wouldn't even be here if it wasn't for Blasko*, Josephine thought, grinding her teeth.

Clarence stood up from his spot on the sofa where he had been embracing a petite, blonde woman and approached Blasko. Josephine remembered her manners and said quickly, "I'm sorry. This is my distant cousin from Romania, Baron Dragomir Blasko."

"I'm Clarence Erickson and this is my wife, Amanda. My sister, Carrie," he said, indicating a tall and wiry woman sitting in a chair in the corner. "I'm sorry, but we're all still in shock."

"I spoke with your sheriff. I was a magistrate back in my country and I've offered my services to help find the one who did this horrible crime," Blasko said. His tone was sad, and he shook his head as he spoke. Josephine was impressed with how he managed to imply so many things that weren't true without actually lying.

"The sheriff said it must have been a stranger," Clarence said.

"Obviously, no one we know would do something... so horrible," Lucy said. "We told him that."

"I would like to see the body," Blasko said bluntly. Everyone stared at him for a moment. Lucy covered her eyes and stifled a cry.

"The sheriff said we should keep everyone out. But I guess if you've spoken with him…" Clarence sounded unsure, but finally said, "I'll show you up." He started to go and his wife reached for his hand. He stopped and turned to her. "I'll be right back." She nodded, but still paused before finally letting go of his hand.

"Thank you," Blasko said and followed Clarence out of the room, leaving Josephine with the three women.

Blasko had smelled the blood as soon as they entered the house. Now, as he followed Clarence up the stairs, the coppery odor became stronger.

Samuel Erickson's room faced the front of the house. Clarence hesitated at the door. "I'd rather not go in."

"I understand," Blasko said, reaching for the doorknob.

Inside the room, the light was on. The body was lying on the bed, arms at its sides. The bludgeoned face was unrecognizable beneath the corpse's blood-soaked grey hair.

Blasko had to struggle against an inner urge as the blood called to him. He fought it down as he looked around the room for clues to the killer. Drops of blood were scattered all around the bed. Looking closely, Blasko could almost see the outline of the killer's shoes, but the image was elusive. As he leaned over, he spied a button lying on the floor just under the bed. He reached down and picked it up. It was bone, drilled with four holes, and with just a few strands of white thread still attached. Blasko carefully placed it in his pocket, then stood back and looked at the body.

The man had been dressed in pants, socks and a dress shirt. His shoes were at the foot of the bed and his coat and waistcoat were folded on a nearby chair. Blasko had seen thousands of men and women killed over the centuries, with every imaginable weapon. Erickson appeared to have been bludgeoned with a rounded object, possibly a metal rod of some sort. But it hadn't been very thick, judging by the indentations in his forehead. There'd been more than a dozen savage strikes to his head and face. He'd been killed early in the attack, but not before his right hand could grasp the sheets in a death grip.

Much of the death Blasko had seen had occurred in battle. A soldier tried to end another's life with as few blows as possible, striking simply to eliminate the foe. This is not the work of a man eliminating a threat. The killing here was out of hatred, Blasko thought to himself.

There were streaks of blood on the quilt where it appeared the murderer had wiped off the weapon. Blasko looked around the room for the weapon, not really believing the killer had been careless enough to leave it there. A fire poker would have been the right size, but the one leaning next to the fireplace near a coal shovel had obviously not been moved in a while. Though it was early October, it still wasn't cold enough to need a fire.

Deciding that he'd seen everything he could in the bedroom, Blasko stood where the killer must have stood by the bed. How did the killer escape? he thought. Trying to imagine himself as the murderer, he turned toward the door. Walking in that direction, he sniffed the air, still smelling blood. He walked out the door and past Clarence, who was leaning against the balustrade and smoking a cigarette.

"Not very pretty, is it?" he said to Blasko, who barely acknowledged him.

Blasko walked down the hall, subtly sniffing the air for the scent of more blood. He got a stronger whiff and looked down to see a spot on the carpet runner that ran the length of the hall. Ten feet farther along, he found another small spot.

Clarence followed him as he moved slowly down the hall. Blasko had expected the trail to turn and go down the stairs, but instead it led to the bathroom door. Opening it revealed a room with a claw-foot tub, a pedestal sink and a toilet with an overhead tank. The floor was covered in tile that extended four feet up the walls. Blasko moved to the sink and examined it. The were still droplets of water around the handles and the drain.

"Has anyone used this since the murder?" Blasko asked, turning to Clarence.

"I don't know," Clarence said with a shrug. "You don't think the killer took the time to wash up, do you?"

Blasko looked at Clarence. "Did your father always lie down in the afternoon?"

"He always did on Wednesdays."

Most businesses in town closed on Wednesday afternoon, partly to make up for Saturday when they worked half a day to accommodate the farmers who came into town to do business, and partly to give folks time to get ready for Wednesday evening church services.

"I have some questions for everyone," Blasko said, heading down the stairs.

Josephine had not been dealing well with the uncomfortable situation in the parlor. All of the women were deep in their own thoughts when Blasko and Clarence came back into the room.

"Please, a few questions if you don't mind," Blasko said, like a flamboyant magician getting ready to perform a trick.

Everyone stared at him.

"What time did Mr. Erickson go upstairs?"

"Same as every Wednesday, I suppose, around two o'clock," Lucy said without any inflection.

"And where was everyone from two o'clock until the body was discovered?"

"Why?" Carrie asked sharply.

Blasko knew better than to cast aspersions on the family, so he tread lightly. "I want to determine when and how the killer slipped into the house. If I know where each of you were, that will give me some idea of the opportunities the man had," he said reasonably.

"Shouldn't this wait for the sheriff?"

"He is off searching for the madman," Blasko said without answering Lucy's question.

"Well, I was out at a friend's," Lucy responded, turning to Josephine. "I went over to Barbara's house. She's been down with the flu, so I took over a pie that Myra had baked."

"When was this?" Blasko asked.

"I left here about noon and got back at four o'clock."

"And the body was discovered…?"

"At six when Samuel didn't come downstairs. I asked Myra to go up and check on him. It wouldn't be the first time he'd overslept. We all heard her scream." Lucy shivered at the memory.

"I see." *How do you know for sure that he went upstairs at two if you weren't here?* Blasko wanted to ask, but he decided now was not the time to start a confrontation.

"Clarence, where were you this afternoon?"

"I was at work. I came home just a little before six."

"Where do you work?"

"I own the Sumter Garage," he said, sounding a bit offended that Blasko didn't know.

"And you?" Blasko turned to the young woman who was clutching her husband tightly.

"I was tending my roses," Amanda said timidly.

Blasko turned to Carrie, who didn't wait for him to form a question.

"I was going over the household accounts in the study. Father turned them over to me a couple of years ago," she said, exchanging a look with her stepmother that Blasko caught out of the corner of his eye.

"No one saw or heard anyone enter the house?"

"We told Sheriff Logan that. Trouble is, anyone could have come in here and gone upstairs without being noticed," Carrie said.

"What about the servants?"

"Myra was running some errands and the cook was busy in the kitchen. Unless she looked out the window, she wouldn't have seen anything. We keep the door to the kitchen closed when the weather is warm to keep the heat from coming into the rest of the house," Lucy said.

"Where is the cook now?"

"She left at five. Alice goes to church on Wednesday evenings at Primitive Baptist. She prepares dinner before she goes and Myra serves it."

There was a knock on the door and Myra came in, looking frightened.

"Mrs. Erickson, Dr. McGuire is here."

Everyone stood up and followed Myra out into the hall, where McGuire was standing, wearing a grim expression. He was holding his black bag and a log book that he used to record deaths in the county.

"Sorry to hear about the trouble," he said to the group, letting his eyes move from one person to the other. "The sooner I can see him, the more accurate my report will be."

"I'll show you up," Clarence said. But before Dr. McGuire could follow him, the front door opened and Deputy Paige walked in.

"Dr. McGuire, I'll show you to the body," he said, pushing past everyone. He gave Clarence a look that seemed to say: Step back, the law's here.

As Paige and McGuire went upstairs, Josephine came in close to Blasko and said sternly, "We can go now."

Blasko looked at her as though he was thinking about arguing. "Very well," he finally said. "I'm deeply sorry for your loss," he told the family and then headed for the door.

The crowd outside was two deep at the sidewalk. Harry Elton, the milk delivery man, was wearing a badge on his flannel shirt and was busy shooing people away from the house. Josephine and Blasko pushed their way through the crowd. A few people greeted Josephine with waves and nods.

"This killer was not a stranger," Blasko said, once they were out of earshot of the gawkers.

"How can you be sure?" Josephine asked skeptically.

Blasko told her what he'd seen upstairs. "The man was killed by someone who hated him. After the assault, the murderer went into the bathroom and cleaned up. Whoever it was knew that household's routine."

CHAPTER NINE

Once back inside Josephine's house, Blasko paced the parlor. "What do you know about the family?"

"Not too much. Erickson was a skinflint, but a good businessman. He and my father were two of the only men in town not hit too hard by the stock market crash and everything that came after."

"What about Clarence?"

Josephine sat down on the sofa. "That's an interesting story. Well, at least the rumors are interesting. Erickson wanted his son to learn about automobiles. With his usual eye for business, he figured they were going to take over from horses, so Erickson wanted to have a son who understood them. It worked too well. Clarence got a job at the garage in town. Story is, he became obsessed with cars, much to his father's irritation.

"Then Clarence and Amanda met at a dance at the veterans' hall. Mr. Erickson disapproved, of course, since she was the daughter of the garage owner. The rumor is that Amanda either got pregnant or pretended to be pregnant so that Clarence's father would let them get married. Whatever the real story, the baby never came. Regardless, Erickson bought the garage from Amanda's father and presented it to the couple as a wedding present.

"That was six years ago. They're living in Erickson's house while they wait on their own house to be built. Another gift from dad. Considering how cheap Erickson was, he couldn't have been very happy about the whole thing, but he kept paying for things anyway."

"And the daughter?"

"You're really trying to figure this out?" Josephine asked. The murder was the first thing that Blasko had seemed really interested in since coming to America. He'd given a certain restless attention to the renovation work in the basement, but no more than he would have given to unpacking in a hotel room.

"I always find death interesting," he said with raised eyebrows. Josephine couldn't tell if he was making a joke or not. "Tell me about Carrie."

"Carrie is older than Clarence. A confirmed spinster. I don't know if she's ever been courted by anyone. Carrie's got a sharp tongue and a quick temper. I think everyone in town has had a run-in with her at one time or another. When I was in school, she called me a harlot for holding hands with a boy as we walked past their house. You don't really think she could have murdered him?"

"Ha, I remember a town we conquered in Turkey back… Well, a long time ago. We had captured the town and chased all the men out. Only the women were left. I'd ordered my warriors to be respectful. Not the normal practice at the time, but we were far from our lines and I didn't need the locals fighting us tooth and nail. My men bedded down for the night. In the morning, I found that half of my regiment had been slaughtered in their beds by the women of the town. A woman can be as savage and as brutal as any man, if driven to it."

"Carrie, maybe, but I don't think you can say that about Amanda Erickson. She's very timid. Kind. I think she has just a small group of friends. Grace might know more. She spends a lot of time with Myra."

"What about the stepmother?"

"Lucy isn't a wicked stepmother. She may be a little too flirtatious for some, but I've never heard any rumors about her. Again, Grace might have heard something from Myra."

Josephine called to Grace. She walked into the room, giving Blasko the evil eye the entire time.

"They ain't locked him up yet?" she said to Josephine, without taking her eyes off of Blasko.

"Don't be silly. I didn't kill that man," Blasko said harshly.

"Ever since Miss Josephine told me about all your... odd habits, I've been warning her. Keep a rattlesnake in your house, you're going to get bit."

Josephine had needed to tell Grace early on about Blasko's feeding habits and issues with sunlight, but she'd only hinted at his age. Even with the extra pay, it had been clear from day one that spending time in the house with Blasko and keeping his secrets was going to be a challenge for Grace.

"He didn't kill Erickson, and he's... probably not dangerous," Josephine said, with just the hint of a smile in her voice.

"This ain't funny," Grace said. "There's a murderer on the loose." If possible, she stared even harder at Blasko.

"Exactly! That's why I'm trying to find out who the killer is," Blasko said, joining in on the staring contest.

"Grace, the baron has some law enforcement experience and he wants to find out some things about the Erickson household. We thought you would be the best person to ask."

The compliment caused Grace to retreat a little from her defensive posture. "I don't gossip," she began, then relented. "Now Myra, she does talk."

"We just want to know if there's any... tension in the house," Josephine said.

"Oh, there's some tension." She paused. "At least that's what Myra says."

"Clarence and Mr. Erickson didn't get along?" Blasko asked.

"Myra says Mr. Erickson said that Mr. Clarence was a disgrace to the family."

"Why would he say that?" Blasko followed up.

"I guess 'cause he didn't like havin' a son who was more interested in tinkerin' with those old cars than runnin' all Mr. Erickson's other businesses."

"What did Clarence think of his father?"

"Called him an old skinflint. He wanted to move out, but Miss Amanda doesn't want to move until their house is finished. They've had some real arguments."

"What does Myra think of Clarence?"

"She says there's something funny about him. 'Course, she wasn't his wet nurse. Mamma Rose nursed him after his mother died. Now Rose was old when I was young, so she's gone to sit with the good Lord now. Myra liked him a little better after he married Miss Amanda. Maybe Myra just likes Miss Amanda."

"Myra get along with Lucy?"

"Myra and Mrs. Erickson are on the same side sometimes. Like once, Mrs. Erickson wanted to hire another woman to help with the work, but Mr. Erickson put his foot down and that was the end of that, no matter how much Mrs. Erickson asked him to."

"Did anyone get along with Mr. Erickson?"

"I don't know 'bout get along, but him and Miss Carrie are cut from the same cloth. They got the same temper and miserly ways. However, they sometimes butted heads. Miss Carrie was against buildin' the house and buyin' that garage for Mr. Clarence. I don't know if she was jealous of his havin' a wife or just didn't want to see the money get spent."

"What did Myra think when she saw Mr. Erickson's body?" Blasko asked.

After a long moment, Grace fixed her eyes firmly on Blasko and said, "She thought it was some maniac that come in and killed him."

Blasko waved his hand dismissively. "You know I don't go out during the day."

"I know that's what you say," Grace shot back.

Josephine stepped in. "If you wanted to find out more about what was going on in the Erickson household, who would you talk to, besides Myra?" She was being drawn into the mystery in spite of herself.

"I guess I'd talk to Mr. and Mrs. Kelly. They're over there more than anyone else."

"The Kellys? Really? I didn't realize they were such good friends with the Ericksons." Josephine thought they would make an odd mix. The Kellys were considerably younger than Samuel and Lucy Erickson, and not quite as well off.

"Mrs. Kelly and Miss Amanda were in school together. They were best friends then and that ain't changed."

The room grew quiet as Josephine and Blasko mulled over all this information.

"I got work to do," Grace finally said.

"Of course. Thank you, Grace," Josephine said.

"I know the devil done it," the maid mumbled as she turned and left the room.

"Querulous servant," Blasko muttered at Grace's retreating figure.

"You better be grateful to Grace. She's kept your secrets better than most would have."

"Can you arrange a meeting with the Kellys?"

"Like having them over for dinner?" Josephine asked, a little horrified as her mind brought forth the frightful image of Blasko trying to question them. "I don't think that would be a good idea."

"We need to find out what was going on in that house."

"Maybe the sheriff will catch whoever did it."

"Hah! That man is an imbecile. He's out chasing an imaginary vagabond ax-murderer."

Before Josephine could say anything else, there was a loud knock at the front door.

"What in the world?" Josephine hastened to see who it

was, easily beating Grace to the front door. "I've got this," she told Grace, who shrugged and headed back to the kitchen.

As if summoned by the very mention of his name, Sheriff Logan was standing on the front porch when Josephine opened the door.

"Can I help you?"

"Where's the foreigner? What was he doing questioning the Ericksons? They thought he was working for me or some such nonsense." Logan was literally dancing from one foot to the other. If it had been someone of less social standing blocking the doorway, he would have simply pushed his way past, but manners demanded that he wait for an invitation.

"Perhaps there has been some confusion," Josephine said, backing up and giving Logan room to come through.

Once in the parlor, Logan fixed Blasko with a cold stare, but the foreign man pretended not to notice, frustrating the sheriff even more. Josephine stood back, unsure of which tack the unpredictable Blasko was going to take. Finally, he turned and looked at the sheriff, breaking into his most engaging smile and tilting his head a little to one side.

"I am sorry if there has been some… misunderstanding." Blasko's accent was suddenly much stronger. "My English is not always so good. As an officer of the court in my land, it is a privilege to be observing a man of your experience on such a case," Blasko said with so much honey that Josephine was surprised bears didn't bust into the room and lick him to death.

"Oh, well, sure," Logan stammered. "I was just taken by surprise when the Ericksons said you'd been questioning them."

"I am so sorry. I never meant to… How do you say it? Step on your toes," Blasko said, his face a picture of innocence.

"No harm done," Logan assured him.

"How is the manhunt going? Have you caught the

villain?" Blasko asked, leaning forward as though he expected the sheriff to entertain him with an exciting story of a desperate pursuit and shoot-out.

"We've searched the freight train and the box cars that were in the yard. One long-haul freight got away, though. We sent word down the line to detain the train and anyone on board. Soon as we hear anything, I'll head out that way. Should be able to stop it short of Mobile. Of course, the killer could have jumped from the train anywhere between here and there." Logan enjoyed talking about his police work. He liked a chase a lot better than a mystery, probably because he was a lot better at chasing criminals than detecting them.

"You still think the killer was a stranger?" Josephine asked.

"I do. Can't imagine someone from around here doing anything this cold-blooded." He paused and then added, "Don't get me wrong. We got some mean drunks. They get lickered up, they're liable to do anything. Poor Mrs. Hopkins. I pulled her husband off of her a couple months ago. The woman'd been beat half to death. Floyd Hopkins is harmless until he gets a snoot full. Prohibition hasn't done shi—" He stopped himself, remembering that Josephine was present. "...Anything to stop the drunkards."

"This was no drunk," Josephine said, thinking of the crime scene that Blasko had described, not to mention the stealth and nerve that was required to pull it off.

"You're right there. Gonna be a madman. Someone like the Axeman of New Orleans, I'm thinking." The Axeman had made national news with his penchant for slaughter and jazz.

"I would be honored if you would allow me to observe your handling of the case. I'm sure it will be quite instructive," Blasko said politely.

"Sure, I guess. 'Long as you don't mess with any evidence." Logan was puffed up from the compliments Blasko had lavished on him.

The sheriff said his goodnights and Josephine and Blasko walked him to the door. They followed him out onto the porch and watched him walk across the street and through the crowd that was still gathered outside the Erickson house and gossiping.

The night was cooled by a gentle breeze. In the distance, just over the murmur of the gawkers across the street, Josephine could hear the call of a great horned owl asking: *Who?*

Who indeed? she wondered.

She looked over at Blasko, who was holding his chin high as though he was sniffing the air for clues. *Hell, maybe he is*, Josephine thought.

Though she hated to admit it, there was something about Blasko's military bearing that drew her to him. She couldn't help feeling something deep within herself when she looked at him. She wanted to dismiss it as just their inadvertent blood bond, yet there seemed to be another type of attraction entwined with her emotions. She almost reached out and touched his arm. *Stop it!* she commanded herself. *All I'm feeling is whatever sorcery his blood has worked on me. I will not be drawn closer to him.*

Blasko turned toward her, looking into her eyes as though he'd read her thoughts. It was a long moment before they broke eye contact.

"Can you believe what's happened?" came a high, grating voice from the darkness. The figure of Evangeline Anderson appeared in the soft light cast by the house's windows. The woman was thin with narrow eyes that were constantly looking for something to gossip about. She was only a little older than Josephine and had a son that she smothered. Her husband worked as much as he could at the lumber mill still owned by his father, no doubt in an effort to spend as little time at home as possible.

"Evening, Evie," Josephine said, trying to make her voice as neutral as possible. Her neighbor was a notorious busybody.

"Oh, is that the baron with you?"

"Miss Evangeline," Blasko said, acknowledging her with a slight bow.

She had been stalking the house ever since Blasko had moved in. Even he'd become tired of her popping over whenever she saw him moving about. At first he'd been flattered by her fascination with his title and foreign mannerisms, but it had quickly become tiresome. More than once, Josephine had had to shoo her away from the basement windows. Of course, Evie always had an excuse. Usually she had one of her tasteless pies in hand, claiming that she had made two and wanted to give one to Josephine for her guest. But no one was fooled.

"They say he was beaten to death in his own bed," Evie said, sounding more excited than scandalized.

"Yes, it's very sad," Josephine said, hoping that Evie would go away. The odds on that were long at best.

"I bet the daughter did it. She's mean as a snake," Evie said, clearly referring to Carrie.

"I doubt that. Carrie has her rough edges, but I can't believe she'd kill her own father," Josephine said, annoyed that she felt compelled to defend someone who she personally thought might be capable of murder.

"Had you already met the family?" Evangeline asked Blasko, who'd been trying to ignore the woman.

"Not before tonight," he said, finally turning to look at Evangeline and giving her the full power of his stare until she quickly turned away.

"Did you just get up?" Evie asked, undaunted by her defeat in the staring game. Along with everything else, she'd developed an unnerving interest in Blasko's personal habits. His explanations about his sun allergy had not done much to quell her curiosity.

"No. I've been up since the sun went down. I always get hungry at sunset," he said, trying to catch her eye again. Josephine had warned him not to tease Evie. The goading just made her more determined to spy on him.

"Sheriff Logan thinks the murder is the work of a homicidal maniac," Josephine said, which was true. "He said that everyone should stay in their own homes until the killer is caught," she added, which was certainly not true.

"Oh, I don't think…"

"We'd better get back inside," Josephine said to Blasko.

He looked back at her, clearly weighing his options. For just a second his eyes shifted to Evie. "Yes, you should get to the safety of your own home. The killer could still be in the area," he told her.

"I'm sure Cyril must be terrified," Josephine added.

At the mention of her overgrown man-child, Evangeline glanced around nervously. "Perhaps you're right. I probably should go check on him."

The boy had recently turned eighteen and the rumor was that he'd just stopped sucking his thumb the year before. At one time, Josephine had thought the jokes at the boy's expense were cruel, but as he had become older and even more childish and petulant, she'd quit trying to defend him. *When does a child become responsible for his own behavior?* Josephine wondered.

"You shouldn't bait her," Josephine said to Blasko as they watched Evangeline disappear into the dark.

"I have to have *some* fun," he answered dryly.

"At least it doesn't look like anyone is pointing their finger at you for the murder."

"We'll see," he said, knowing that she was trying to stop him from doing any more investigating and also knowing that he had no intention of stopping. Not now. "I'm going out for a while," he said, heading down the steps from the porch.

"Don't go out tonight."

"I'll be back before sunrise," he said, knowing he was irritating her.

"You're just going to bring suspicion onto yourself," Josephine said to his retreating back.

"Leave this to me." He turned and insolently tipped his

hat to her.

"Ugh," Josephine groaned to herself, half wanting to follow him but knowing that it was impossible. If he wanted to lose her, he could. She'd actually tried to keep up with him one night shortly after they'd arrived from Europe, but in a matter of minutes he'd disappeared into the darkness. Through their blood bond she always had a sense of where he was, but it wasn't enough to follow him. *Just let him go*, she finally told herself and went back inside.

CHAPTER TEN

Blasko moved through the darkness with ease, his night vision as good as that of any predator. Even as he'd lost his ability to move about in daylight or to survive without drinking blood, he'd gained other powers. For decades he'd fought against the reality that he had become a creature of the night, but now he embraced it. Men do their worst at night. Through the centuries, he'd been able to use his unusual skills to defend himself and his people. The thought of his homeland was painful. *They abandoned me long before I left them*, he told himself.

During his nightly excursions, Blasko had gotten a feel for the town of Sumter. It was a quiet place, made up of working men and women who turned in early so they could rise before the first light of day. The town was only a dozen blocks wide and twice as many long, making it easy for Blasko to also wander the woods and countryside surrounding it. This land was so gentle compared to the rocky crags and hard-scrabble farmland of his ancestral mountains. Walking the woods and country roads of southern Alabama had become one of the real pleasures he'd discovered since moving to this new world.

Blasko was looking for someone—a man he'd talked to

several times, someone that he knew might be useful someday. He knew he'd find Matthew Hodge somewhere near the stores downtown. Matthew was a homeless alcoholic whose only meals came from the scraps the stores threw out before closing. Sure enough, Blasko smelled him from a block away.

Matthew was lying in the alley behind the bakery, leaning against a wooden fence and snoring lightly. Blasko looked down at the man. He was forty years old, wearing an old suit long gone to rags. Beside him was a brown wool blanket made into a bundle that held his few possessions.

"Wake," Blasko said in a normal tone of voice.

At first it didn't appear that the man had noticed, but slowly one eye opened. Then the other flew open and Matthew peered at Blasko, trying to get a good look at him through the fog of drink and the dim light cast by a distant street lamp.

"Mr. Baron, that you?"

"Yes."

"Well, now. What an honor."

Matthew tried to stand, but his left leg was asleep and his equilibrium was still lost in the last bottle he'd drunk. He would have fallen if Blasko hadn't grabbed his arm.

"Easy."

"Thank you. One old soldier to another, huh?" Matthew mumbled.

"Come with me," Blasko said, picking up the man's bundle with one hand while using his other to half carry Matthew up the block to Main Street. There was a horse trough there and he eased the man down beside it. "Clean yourself up."

Matthew looked at Blasko for a moment, then he stripped off his coat and shirt. A quick wash and the cool night air helped, if not to sober him, then to at least make him more conscious.

"So what's up, Shadow? That's who you remind me of, the Shadow. 'Who knows what evil lurks in the hearts of men.'" Matthew stumbled over to a bench and sat down heavily, looking up at Blasko.

Blasko watched him with studied interest. "I need your help," he finally said.

"Damn, you must be in trouble if you need my help," Matthew said with a laugh, almost falling over in his seat.

"There's been a murder."

"Come on, don't make fun of me. I was just joking calling you the Shadow. Let's just have a nice talk like we have before."

Blasko had spoken with the man on several occasions during his explorations of Sumter. Matthew had shared a little about his life and service in the Great War. He'd told Blasko about his regiment's fight in the Belleau Woods and how, when he'd returned home, he'd found that his wife had run off with a sailor.

"Mr. Erickson has been murdered," Blasko blurted.

Matthew stared at Blasko, trying to decide if he was playing a prank on him. Matthew was used to that. As the town drunk, he'd been the butt of more than one joke.

"Really? Who done it?"

"Precisely the point."

Matthew's eyes got big. "Hey! I never hurt no one that wasn't wearing a German uniform. I didn't do nothin'. I haven't even seen—"

Blasko held up his hand. "I know that you didn't kill him. I need your help to find out who did."

"You're crazy. I'm a fu… A damn drunk," Matthew said, looking down at the ground.

"You don't have to be."

Something in Blasko's voice caused Matthew to look up. "Whatta you mean? I've tried quitting. Not so damn easy. I'll quit! I've said it a million times and meant it each one, but here I am." He spread his hands and presented his disheveled appearance.

"I can help you," Blasko said. "But I want something in return."

Matthew began to laugh and turned out all his pockets. "Take all my money," he said, laughing more loudly. "You're something else. You'd get more money from a skunk. And he'd smell better."

Matthew was roaring with laughter now at his own expense. Blasko just stood and watched the man until the laughter turned into a coughing fit and finally died away.

"I need you to remain on the streets and to be my eyes and ears."

"I think you are loony."

"Do you want to be sober?"

"Yeah, sure. But not enough to give up drink. Hell, Prohibition hasn't even slowed me down," Matthew said, sounding irritated at the question.

Blasko took a shiny object from his pocket and Matthew's eyes were drawn to it. Blasko showed him a strange gold coin.

"I can make you forget your hunger for drink," Blasko said, twirling the coin in his fingers. As the coin went round and round, it caught the light of the street lamp, flashing in Matthew's eyes.

"I seen a guy when I was in France. Hypnogist or something like that. Made a soldier bark like a dog." Matthew's voice was quiet. He had begun to realize that there was something strange and profound about the dark figure standing over him.

"That is the idea. But instead of barking like a dog, I can make you not want to drink alcohol. Ever. But this must be something you want."

Matthew stared at him. He needed to be sober, he knew that. But a voice inside his head reminded him that the only happiness he got these days was at the bottom of a mason jar of moonshine or a bottle of bathtub gin.

"I guess I could find other things to make me feel good," he mumbled to himself. "I could maybe... meet someone. I haven't been with a woman in... I don't remember." Matthew's head hurt—the concept of being sober seemed overwhelming. He looked at Blasko. "Are you the devil or something?"

"No. But I can grant you this one wish if you want it."

Something in the way Blasko made the offer reminded Matthew of a story he'd heard a long time ago. The people in the story found an object that would grant them their dearest wish, but when the wish became real, the people lived to regret it.

"How long have I got to make up my mind?"

"If you have to decide, then I already have my answer," Blasko said and began to walk away.

Before he could get far, Matthew stood up and shouted. "No! Don't go. I want it," he said in a determined voice.

Blasko turned and looked back at the man, who swayed slightly on his feet.

"Okay. Sit down," he said, moving quickly toward Matthew, who stumbled back onto the bench in the wake of the unexpected advance. The baron sat down next to him so that they were eye to eye. Blasko lifted the coin, holding it in front of Matthew's face. The gold glittered seductively.

The coin was one of hundreds that had lined the bottom of the box he had traveled in from Romania. There was power in the gold that, when mixed with a bit of his native earth, allowed him to cross running water without too much suffering. Since the trip, he'd used many of the coins to pay for the renovations to Josephine's basement, but there were still quite a few remaining.

Blasko began to twirl the coin rhythmically between his fingers while talking in a calm and soothing voice. A trained hypnotist could only hope to mesmerize a subject as deeply as Blasko could. It was another gift that came hand in hand with the curse.

"You are going to surrender control to me," he said in a soft yet commanding tone. "You will open yourself up to the power of my words. You will no longer control your own mind. You will no longer control your own body. I am in control. Not you. I am the one who will tell you what you want. I will tell you what you crave. You will have no desire that is not mine…" Blasko's voice continued in a comforting, yet demanding, drone. Matthew nodded his head dutifully.

"You will never desire alcohol again. If someone mentions beer, you will feel sick. Talking about gin will make your stomach turn until you retch. The smell of alcohol will repulse you. It will be impossible to force liquor past your lips." The litany continued for several minutes before Blasko began the process of bringing Matthew out of the trance.

When Blasko finally put the coin away, Matthew blinked and shook his head. "What'd you do?"

"You'll never be drunk again," Blasko stated.

"That's crazy. I've been drinking since I was twelve. If I want a bottle of gin…" Through the dim light, Blasko watched as Matthew's face turned green and he dry-heaved off the side of the bench. Wiping his eyes, he looked at Blasko with an expression both of anger and wonder. "I really can't drink?"

"No," Blasko responded.

Keeping one eye on Blasko, Matthew took his bundle and unrolled it. Inside was a small flask. Still watching Blasko, he uncorked the bottle. He had planned to raise it to his lips, but as soon as the smell of the homemade gin reached his nostrils his arm jerked, flinging the bottle away. Matthew stared at his hand, shocked that it had seemingly reacted without his consent. "I'll be damned," he whispered.

"No. You are cured," Blasko said with more than a hint of ego.

"Oh, crap. I got dried out once before and the DTs were something awful," Matthew said, his eyes pleading.

"You won't experience anything like that. I took care of it."

"But how…?"

"When you were under my control, I told your mind to ignore any of the physical symptoms. You can relax now." Blasko's tone was brusque. He wanted to get past this and down to the matter at hand. "I need you to tell me everything you know about the Erickson household."

"Oh, yeah," Matthew said, surprised at how clear his mind already seemed without the desire for alcohol clouding his thoughts. "I been hanging out in the alley behind their house a bunch. The garbage from the rich folks' houses is the best. Lots of leftovers. They don't even send it out to the dogs. Erickson's ain't the best. The house on the other side of the alley throws away a lot better grub."

"Never mind the epicurean tour. Have you seen anything unusual there? Think about people coming and going. What have you witnessed that seemed odd or out of place?" Blasko asked, using a soothing cadence. He could have questioned Matthew while he was mesmerized, but Blasko had learned long ago that people in that state were too open to suggestion. When he had tried it on prisoners of war, it had only resulted in things he already knew or suspected being fed back to him.

"Unusual?" Matthew seemed to ponder the question. "There's certainly lots of coming and going, I know that." He got quiet for a minute. "You know, there *is* one thing you probably don't know... One of the places I got my hooch from."

"Hooch?" Blasko asked.

"Corn, moonshine mostly, sometimes bathtub gin. Clarence sells it out of his garage. Rumor has it he's got some friends who run it up from Florida. I only get the cheap stuff, but I hear tell he gets some first-class wares from Florida."

Blasko knew enough to understand this was a big deal. Half of the country's law enforcement was focused on ending the production, importation and sale of alcohol. If Clarence was running rum, he was taking a huge risk.

"Did Erickson know what his son was doing?"

"You got me there. I never saw the old man around the garage. Of course, if he was involved then he wouldn't be around when the deals were going down."

Blasko sighed, realizing this could open up the suspect list to include the kinds of criminals straight out of the movies. Josephine had recently taken Blasko to see a Jimmy Cagney movie and, from what he'd read in the papers, the movie wasn't far from the truth. Erickson might have stepped on the toes of some gang. His murder was certainly vicious enough.

"What about the women? Did you ever see them doing anything unusual? Maybe you saw one of them someplace you didn't expect her to be."

Blasko was hoping to take advantage of the village drunk's position as part of the scenery. No one paid him any attention. At first, people would avoid eye contact so they didn't feel compelled to talk to him or give him spare change. After a while, they'd walk past him at a faster pace to avoid the odor. Soon they wouldn't be able to remember seeing him even when they tried.

"I run whenever I see that old spinster. I was sleeping out in the alley behind their house one day about a year ago. I guess she was walking by and I woke up and scared her. She tore me up with her umbrella. Called me words I haven't heard since the Army. Wouldn't want to get on her bad side."

"What about the younger woman?"

"You mean the one married to Clarence? I seen her at the garage a few times."

"Does she know about the liquor?"

"Couldn't say. I don't think she was ever there when I was buying. 'Course, I get pretty excited when I'm getting my squeeze." As soon as he said this, Matthew rubbed his gut and looked uncomfortable. "What did you do to me?" he asked, not sounding like he really wanted to know.

Blasko ignored him. "And Mrs. Erickson?"

"Lady Lucy," Matthew said with a strange inflection.

"What about her?" Blasko pressed.

"Nothing. I've just met her a couple times. She hangs around the house mostly. Hey, I remember! I seen her and the old man arguing one day. Their car had broken down. She said he should buy a new one, but he said Clarence could fix it. Said he'd make Clarence come home from the garage and get it running again."

"That's all?"

Matthew shrugged. "She shut up after that."

"Fine, that's enough for now." Blasko looked at Matthew, wondering if he'd made the right decision. "You remember what you promised me in exchange for your sobriety?" he asked.

For a moment it looked like Matthew didn't know what he was talking about. Slowly, though, his eyes narrowed and his expression darkened. "I guess I do. You said that I should be your eyes and ears. Or somethin'." He looked around as if he wished he had a bottle.

"You are going to be completely sober tomorrow morning. How long has it been since you had a day without a drink?"

"You mean beer or nothin'? Probably when I was in the Army. What's that, almost fifteen years?"

"You will do what you always do, but you'll do it sober. Don't tell anyone about this. I want you to watch everyone. I want you to hear everything."

"Hell, what if I don't want to?" Matthew asked petulantly.

"Anything I do, I can undo. Is that clear? Do this for me, and there will be more rewards to come," Blasko told him. He wasn't exactly sure what he would be able to do for the man, but he needed to provide some incentive—both the whip and the carrot.

"Yeah, okay. How long?"

"The more information you can get for me, the sooner you will be able to get on with your life. A life I am giving to you, I might add."

"I get that."

"I'll see you tomorrow after dark. Keep an eye on Clarence and Amanda, as well as Lucy and Carrie."

"Yes, sir," Matthew said, giving Blasko an ironic salute as he walked away. "Hey, how'm I goin' to spend my time if I can't drink?" he yelled to the retreating figure.

Ignoring Matthew, Blasko headed back toward the Ericksons' house. When he arrived, the body was being hauled out to the hearse parked at the curb. The crowd spread out just enough to make room for the doctor and the morticians to get the body through. A white sheet covered the corpse, blood seeping through to the vicarious thrill of the gawkers.

Blasko stood back and watched. Lucy and Amanda looked distraught as they stood on the porch, watching as their husband and father-in-law was carried down the walk. Clarence came out and talked with them for a moment before they all went back into the house.

Blasko's attention was caught by a middle-aged man standing with the crowd in front of the house. Unlike everyone else whose attention was focused on the body, the man was watching the women on the porch, a fedora pulled down low over his face.

As soon as the women went back inside, the man turned and walked away. Blasko quietly followed him. The man looked around a couple of times as though he was afraid he might be noticed. After he'd walked at least a block, he pulled his hat up and walked more quickly.

Blasko followed him over three blocks to a large brick home. A '28 Buick was parked in the drive and the lights were on in the house. The man stopped and leaned against the car. Blasko watched him as the man smoked a cigarette before going into the house.

Blasko moved closer and could hear voices coming from inside the house. The scent of a woman reached him, but he couldn't detect signs of any children. Soon, the lights began to go off in the house until only one room was illuminated. Finally, that light also went out.

Blasko made a note of the address before walking home. *Which of the women had he been looking at?* Blasko wondered.

Why didn't he want to be seen? He could think of several reasons.

It was past one in the morning by the time he arrived back at Josephine's house. He'd had a separate entryway built so that he could access his basement apartment directly from the outside without disturbing anyone else in the house.

Once inside, Blasko picked up a copy of the *Adventures of Sherlock Holmes* and tried to concentrate on the story he was reading. But he couldn't keep his mind from thinking of Josephine. He recognized the pull of the blood they shared, but there was something else, something that scared him. She had a quality about her that he hadn't seen in a woman in many years.

There was a rustle from the rafters and a small bat fluttered down to land on Blasko's arm

"Vasile, my friend, what do you think? Do you have a female bat that you visit in the night? It's been more than fifty years, locked up in my fortress in the mountains, since I've been with a woman. But they have not gotten any easier to understand, my friend."

The bat simply looked at him and nuzzled Blasko's finger. He'd found the creature lying on the ground, stunned, during one of his nightly walks. His castle in Romania had a been a home for many such creatures and he had always found them pleasant companions. So he'd brought this one home and fed it insects, nursing it back to health.

"What am I to do, little one? I thought I was through with this world. Now I'm chained to that... woman. There are times I think she wishes I was deader than I am," he said, lightly stroking the bat's head. Vasile shook his ears as though Blasko's touch tickled him, then curled up on his shoulder. Blasko sighed and went back to his book.

CHAPTER ELEVEN

Josephine woke up at five. She tossed and turned, wanting to go back to sleep, but knowing that she should go down to the basement and speak with Blasko before he went to bed. *No, before he goes to coffin*, she corrected herself, still surprised at how the abnormal had slowly become normal.

Still dressed in her nightgown, she put on a robe and went quietly down the stairs. The mornings were noticeably cooler now that it was almost fall. She rapped three times on the basement door.

"Good morning," he greeted her as he led her into his parlor. "I'm glad you came."

Josephine had read him the riot act after the second time he'd knocked on her door in the middle of the night, wanting to talk. Since then, he'd made of point of letting her know she was always welcome to visit him in the predawn hours.

She spoke quickly before losing her nerve. "I don't know if investigating the murder is the right thing to do. No one seems to be pointing the finger at you." Josephine regretted letting Blasko get involved and had been replaying events over and over in her mind most of the night, trying to come up with a way to talk him into backing off.

"They will. If the sheriff doesn't find a suspect soon, he will quickly look for another person to cast aspersions on. At some point, they will start going through the list of strangers in town. No, I'm going to solve this."

She looked down at the volume of *Sherlock Holmes* on the end table and frowned. "Being the high sheriff or judge or whatever you were in Romania doesn't give you any experience with our system of justice."

"A good detective uses the same methods no matter what country he is in."

"Reading books and torturing peasants doesn't make you a detective," Josephine snapped back. *Why does he get my goat every time we have a discussion?* she asked herself.

"Bah!" he muttered, too indignant to come up with a better response. He was now determined to catch the killer, if for no other reason than to prove to this insolent woman that he knew what he was doing.

Josephine saw the look in his eye and figured she might have pushed him a little far. With a sigh, she decided to offer an olive branch. "Okay, look into it. But don't be too obvious."

"It would be easier with your help. You can go places I can't."

"Like out in the sunshine?"

"Exactly. But more to the point, you are friends with these people."

"I'm not exactly friends with—"

"Maybe not friends, but neighbors. Point being, they accept you as one of their own."

"Maybe." Most of her childhood friends had moved on to lives filled with husbands, households and children. Only her father's position in the town had kept her involved in the social circles she'd grown up with.

"Arrange a dinner party with the Kellys."

"I still don't think that's a great idea," she demurred,

"Of course, I can just go off on my own. I'm sure I can find out what I need to by myself," Blasko said, turning away from her and hoping the threat would be enough to cause her to capitulate.

"Fine, you win. I'll arrange the dinner. I'd prefer to keep an eye on you." She couldn't afford for him to get entangled in a web that might expose what he really was.

They talked for a few more minutes about housekeeping issues before she left, wondering as she had every day since they'd returned from Romania how this was all going to end.

Josephine went into the kitchen for breakfast. She'd been taking breakfast and lunch in the kitchen ever since her father had died. It just didn't make sense for Grace to cart everything back and forth to the dining room just for her.

As soon as Josephine entered the kitchen, Anna, the cook, started frying eggs and bacon. The *Sumter Times* was on the table. Emmett Wolfe and his staff must have stayed up all night to get the murder into the morning edition. The headline read: *Erickson Murdered*. Other papers would have printed a more colorful headline, but Emmett was diligent in his journalistic responsibilities. During the banking crisis, Josephine had once heard him tell her father that he wasn't going to print anything that would add to the panic, knowing if the town went to hell then everyone would go down into the inferno with it.

As Josephine ate her breakfast and read the paper, Grace kept coming through and giving her looks. Josephine knew Grace wanted to talk about the night before, but since they'd agreed not to tell Anna too much about Blasko, Grace had to wait.

"I got the stew going. I'm going to do some baking out in the summer kitchen. Grace can keep an eye on this." Anna indicated the pot of stew on the stove.

"Thank you, Anna," Josephine said, looking up in surprise to see the cook still standing beside her.

Normally, Anna would have already headed for the door. At sixty years old, Anna kept pretty much to herself. She was from New Orleans, of French and Spanish descent. She'd shown up in town with her husband twenty years ago with little money. Her husband had gotten a job as a butcher while Josephine's father had hired Anna as a cook. The few times that Josephine had tried to get her to talk about her family, Anna had told her she didn't have any family left. Never had Anna mentioned anything about her life before moving to Sumter. In fact, she seldom talked about anything. This morning was different. She clearly had something on her mind.

"Is something wrong?" Josephine asked her, putting down the paper.

"Yes." Anna hesitated. "The murder." Anna worriedly pushed back a stray strand of grey hair from her forehead. "Mr. Durand didn't want me coming to work this morning. The murder happening so close." Anna always referred to her husband as Mr. Durand.

"I don't think there is anything to be scared of. I think the murderer wanted to kill Mr. Erickson."

"That's what they thought when the Axeman was killing people. They tried to find out why he was killing the people he was killing. My papa said, 'He's crazy, that's why.' Turned out, Papa was right," Anna said.

Josephine realized she couldn't argue with that logic. The truth was, no one yet knew the motivation in this case.

"Did the Axeman kill anyone during the day?" Josephine asked, already knowing the answer.

"No."

"Okay, so just make sure you leave here when you still have plenty of time to get home safely before the sun goes down. And don't come in until daylight. I certainly don't want you to be in any danger."

Josephine didn't point out that the Axeman of New Orleans killed couples asleep in their own homes. If this murderer was anything like the Axeman, then Anna would be safer at work than at home. But she wasn't going to confuse the poor woman.

Anna nodded. "That makes sense. Thank you, Miss Josephine. I'll leave at six tonight and come in at eight tomorrow, if that's okay."

"That's fine."

Anna, looking more like her usual serene self, headed out to the summer kitchen. No sooner had the screen door banged shut behind her than Grace came bustling into the kitchen.

"You need to tell the sheriff about that man in the basement," Grace said in a conspiratorial whisper.

"The baron had nothing to do with the murder. In fact, he's trying to find out who did do it." Josephine didn't know why she added the last part. She didn't really think Blasko was going to have much luck.

"He ain't right," Grace said, shaking her head. Josephine's explanation for Blasko had been that he had an illness that made him allergic to the sun, and he needed blood due to severe anemia. At first, with modern medicine discovering new diseases and cures almost daily, this had seemed plausible to Grace. But, with time, she had become more and more suspicious of Blasko and his habits. He didn't help the situation by teasing her whenever he had the chance.

"I won't argue with you," Josephine said.

"That blood-drinkin' is like something the devil himself would do," Grace said, not ready to give up on Blasko as a suspect. "I won't do nothin' that's goin' to get between me and God."

"I promise you, the baron is not a devil worshiper," Josephine told her with as much conviction as she could muster.

"I'm just sayin'." Grace shook her head. Their employer-employee relationship had become more of a co-conspirator one since they had started sharing Blasko's secrets.

"I understand your concerns. Trust me."

"But if he's not the killer... Do you really think he can find the monster that did this? Maybe it takes a devil to catch a devil."

"I don't know," Josephine said honestly. "I'm going to help him all I can." The words were out of her mouth before she could stop them, even though she still wasn't sure she should commit herself to being Sancho Panza on Blasko's Quixotic quest. *Are we just going to get ourselves into trouble?* Josephine asked herself.

With Grace temporarily mollified, Josephine pondered her day. Now that she'd agreed to it, she needed to arrange dinner with the Kellys. She looked at the phone. Calling would just be awkward, plus it would give Dolly Garner, the town operator, an opportunity to listen in and develop some gossip to pass on. It would be better to go talk to them in person. She heard the parlor clock chime ten. By the time she got dressed and walked over to the Kellys, it would be a proper hour for a social call.

The Kellys lived three streets over and five blocks north. The homes in the neighborhood were all comfortable and well maintained, with most of the folks who lived there being merchants or professionals. The Kellys' house was a brick, Federal-style home that had been built ten years earlier when the good times looked like they would never end. But the house looked a little out of place mixed in with all the other more popular, Craftsman-style homes. *Trying too hard*, Josephine thought as she walked up the brick steps to the front door.

The walk over had been pleasant, the air cool and dry. Josephine knocked on the door and waited. It took a couple more tries before it finally opened. Sarah Kelly stood in the doorway and looked more than a little surprised to see Josephine standing there.

"Good morning," Josephine said, trying to appear friendly, but also a little downcast out of respect for Mr. Erickson's death.

"Miss Nicolson?"

"Now, Sarah, you should just call me Josephine. Your sister and I were in school together." Josephine felt disingenuous pretending to be an old friend. In truth, she and Tricia, Sarah's sister, had not been close. Tricia had been all about the boys while Josephine was trying to get the best grades she could.

"Well, okay, sure. I was so sorry to hear about your father," Sarah said, making Josephine feel even worse as they walked into the parlor.

"Thank you. And I wanted to offer my condolences about the... sad events of last night. I know you and the Ericksons are good friends."

"Actually, we're more friends with Clarence and Amanda," Sarah said, and Josephine saw a flash of emotion surface for a moment behind Sarah's eyes. Sadness, anger, envy, fear? She couldn't tell.

"Do you know any more about what happened?" Sarah asked her. "We've just read the papers and heard the rumors, but your house is right across the street."

"We did go over and sit with the family for a while last night," Josephine said.

"How horrible for them. The paper said that he was murdered in his bed."

"Yes."

"How did the killer sneak in at night? I always assumed Mr. Erickson's bedroom was on the second floor."

"It is. Actually, he was killed while taking his afternoon nap," Josephine said, watching Sarah closely.

"Just horrible. Not that Mr. Erickson was a very pleasant man, but to be killed like that... You said *we* went over to the house?"

"I have a distant relative from Romania staying with me."

"Oh, yes, I'd heard that. He sounds very interesting."

"Why don't you all come over for dinner tonight? You can meet him," Josephine suggested.

"I don't know... Gosh, we normally play pinochle at the Ericksons' on Thursday nights. Obviously, they won't be up to that this evening. Maybe it would be good to have something else to do tonight. Otherwise, Thomas will worry me to death. He was very upset about the murder. Told me twice this morning to make sure the doors were locked. I'll have to check with him, but that does sound nice."

"Say seven-thirty? I know that's early, but my cook is worried about the murder too, so I told her she could leave early."

Josephine had to do the math. She'd become almost as attuned to sunset as Blasko. Anna would be able to leave early, Grace could keep the food warmed and do any of the last-minute preparations, while Josephine would be able to get Blasko up in time to be dressed and ready to meet the guests by the time the sun had dropped below the trees.

"I'll check with Thomas when he comes home for lunch and let you know," Sarah said.

They chatted a little while longer before Josephine made her excuses and headed for the door. She now had a list of chores to accomplish in order to be ready for dinner that night.

"Dinner?" Anna exclaimed when Josephine finally returned home, her arms full of groceries.

"I'm sorry. I should have warned you this morning. But I've bought everything you'll need. It doesn't need to be anything complicated. A roast with vegetables."

"I guess. That stew'll be better if it sets a day, anyway. I made a pie y'all can have for dessert. Grace can make the biscuits," Anna said, talking as much to herself as to Josephine.

Grace wasn't thrilled, but the idea of getting to see more folks connected, even just barely, to the murder was a lure.

CHAPTER TWELVE

Josephine knocked on Blasko's door at six o'clock. A couple minutes of pounding finally resulted in the door being opened by a somnolent Blasko still wearing his housecoat.

"Yes?" he said sleepily.

"I swear you're as bad as a child at waking up. The Kellys are coming for dinner. You have about an hour to get ready," Josephine told him.

"Excellent." Blasko was suddenly wide awake. He looked at the wristwatch he'd bought a couple of months ago, the first one he'd ever owned, then abruptly closed the door in Josephine's face.

"You're welcome!" she shouted.

The door opened again and, for a moment, Josephine thought Blasko might apologize for his rude behavior. Instead he asked, "Black tie?"

"No," she said, remembering how hard it had been for him to adjust to the more casual atmosphere of America in the 1930s.

"I see." And he closed the door again.

At seven on the dot, Blasko came up the stairs. Josephine *did* admire his punctuality. He was dressed in a dark pinstripe suit and his hair was slicked back. His shoes could have been used as mirrors.

Blasko bowed slightly to Josephine as she came into the hallway. The setting sun cast a faint reddish glow through the front windows. Her knee-length dress, a dark blue satin accented with black sequins, sparkled and highlighted her eyes.

"You look beautiful," Blasko complimented her.

Josephine was warmed by his smile. She gave him a bashful grin and said, "I do look good, don't I?"

"Shall I make you a drink?" he asked, walking over to the bar in the parlor.

"Yes. I think I'm going to need it before the night is over."

Blasko pushed aside the small drinks trolley, which held only mixers, and opened a section of wainscoting behind it to reveal a dozen bottles of liquor. Most of it was still the good stuff that Josephine's father had bought years ago before Prohibition. He'd had the hidden compartment constructed behind the bar, and a much larger one in the floor of the summer kitchen to hold the rest of the supply.

"You tried to explain it to me once, but of all the things this country could have done, I'll never understand why you banned alcohol."

"It's the do-gooder syndrome. Alcohol caused some problems. Drunken men beat their wives and children. Alcoholics were destroying their livers and wasting their lives away. Drunks caused train wrecks and work accidents, et cetera, et cetera. So a bunch of people with their hearts in the right place decided that all we needed to do was to get rid of alcohol. On paper, it makes sense. If you get rid of the alcohol, then people can't drink it. If they can't drink it, then they can't get drunk. If they can't get drunk, then they won't beat their families, wreck trains or destroy their own livers. How could you argue with it? So the Temperance Movement pushed it on the politicians. 'Do you hate families?' they asked. 'Do you want the babies to suffer?' Bam! Next thing you know, we have the Eighteenth Amendment."

"But it didn't get rid of the alcohol," Blasko said as he poured gin into a glass for Josephine.

"Of course it didn't. By all accounts, more people drink now than ever before. But now we have the addition of gangsters, mobsters and more corrupt government agents and police."

Blasko handed the glass to Josephine and she held it up to him in a salute before taking a sip.

"Honestly, I don't know why we don't apply the same rule to laws that we do to investments. If it sounds too good to be true, then it probably is. Of course, the Twenties proved we weren't very good at investing either," Josephine said wryly.

"Politicians will do what politicians will do," Blasko said, dismissing them with a wave of his hand.

"Unfortunately, the rest of us have to live with the consequences."

"You can vote now, right?"

"Yes, women got the vote thirteen years ago."

"So now you can share the blame."

"That's about how much good it's done us," Josephine agreed.

There was a knock at the door, followed by Grace's appearance in the parlor. "The Kellys are here," she announced.

As soon as the couple came through the parlor door, Blasko had to fight back an expression of surprise. Thomas Kelly was the man whom he'd followed home from the Ericksons' the night before.

"You're the fellow from Romania," Thomas said, extending his hand as he walked toward Blasko.

"Baron Dragomir Blasko at your service," he said with a slight bow and click of his heels.

"Thomas Kelly. This is my wife, Sarah."

Blasko took her hand and raised it to his lips. After releasing it, he said, "Honored to meet you, Mrs. Kelly. I know you both are grieving for your friend and neighbor."

"Horrible, just horrible," Thomas said, a little too loudly. "Can't imagine who would do such a thing. I know that Amanda and Clarence must be awfully broke up about it."

"Have you spoken with them?" Josephine interjected.

"I stopped by and spoke with Clarence. I guess Sarah told you, this would have been our usual night to get up with them for our weekly pinochle game. I knew they wouldn't want to play tonight, but I felt I should touch base with them." The explanation seemed overly long.

"Very interesting," Blasko said opaquely.

"Don't know about interesting," Thomas responded, giving Blasko an inquisitive look. "They were all very upset."

"You saw Amanda as well?" Josephine asked.

"Just for a second. She was really too broken up to speak," he said, receiving a sharp glance from Sarah.

"Forgive me. I shouldn't have brought all of this up," Blasko said.

"He's right," Josephine said as Grace, right on cue, came in to announce dinner.

Josephine had helped Grace take the leaves out of the dining room table, so when the four of them sat down it was quite an intimate atmosphere. After a few minutes of savoring the food, the conversation started up again.

"So, Baron, what did you do in Romania?" Sarah asked lightly. "Or don't you noblemen have to work for a living?"

"I had many civic duties," Blasko said.

"What's that mean?"

"It means that he had governmental responsibilities. European nobility often act as judges or local militia leaders," Thomas told her condescendingly.

"I asked the baron," Sarah snapped at her husband.

"It is true. I was a magistrate and commander of a legion when necessary," Blasko said, watching the couple fight a silent battle with their eyes.

"More chicken?" Josephine asked, not really wanting to watch an open fight. The Kellys both waved her off, but took the hint and went back to eating the food on their plates.

"What do you do, Mr. Kelly?" Blasko asked. He was picking at the food on his plate to be polite. He could eat, but it gave him no nourishment.

"I own most of the warehouses down at the river. We store the cotton and load it on the trains. Used to all go out by steamboat down the river to Apalachicola in my father's day. Now we put it on the train."

"There used to be a little dock down there," Josephine added.

"It's still called Cotton Dock. Lots of gambling used to go on down there back in the day," Thomas said.

"And other things," Sarah said cryptically.

"A couple of the old bars are still standing, but they've been flooded a couple times since they were abandoned."

"Funny, I remember my father talking about those bars. He said that's where Mr. Erickson got his start," Josephine said.

Thomas nodded. "I first got to know him when I was buying one of my warehouses. He sure had some stories about the heydays when the boats would come in and all the wild times at the docks. Said the sheriff practically lived down there, between breaking up fights and making sure the drunks didn't drown in the river."

"That was old Sheriff Griffin. Logan took over after him," Josephine explained to Blasko.

"Rumor is that Griffin retired when most of Cotton Dock shut down after Prohibition. Figured if the drinking, gambling and… other things couldn't go on down there, then he wouldn't be able to run his protection racket anymore."

"He should have held on. He could be runnin' 'shine and making more money than ever." Josephine smiled.

"You're about right there."

"One thing about Sheriff Logan, he's honest," Josephine said. "But I think he's got his hands full with this murder."

"Seeing Mr. Erickson last night, I can't help but wonder

who could have committed such a brutal crime," Blasko said.

"Some hobo. Probably rode in on the rails yesterday and was gone by the time they found the poor man," Thomas said, not looking up from his plate. Sarah's head nodded slightly in agreement.

It would appear they see eye to eye about that, at least, Blasko thought. Aloud he said, "But why would a… hobo… want to kill Mr. Erickson?"

"How would I know? A lot of them aren't right in the head. We get them wandering into the warehouse all the time. They always say they're lookin' for work. A handout is what they want. Stink of liquor, most of them. When you tell 'em to go away, they get mad. Maybe Erickson didn't give some guy a handout and the creep followed him home and killed him. Wouldn't put it past most of them. A year ago, one of my guys found a bum down by the tracks with a knife buried in his gut. Stiff as a board."

"Thomas!" Sarah rebuked him.

He looked over at her. "Yeah, sorry. Guess that isn't very polite dinner talk."

"You said you'd met Erickson when you bought the warehouse? I think my father was involved in that transaction," Josephine mentioned.

"He was. I always appreciated his help with my business."

"Of course, I went to school with Mandy," Sarah said, rather out of context. "She was one of my best friends."

Was? wondered Josephine. "Was Clarence in school with you all?" she asked.

"He was several years ahead of us," Sarah answered. "We didn't really know him then."

"He played baseball. I think that's all that kept him in school. Not really the intellectual type," Thomas added.

"That's not fair."

"But true. You know it," Thomas said stiffly.

Blasko carefully watched Thomas and Sarah, observing the coldness between them. Was it simply a normal husband-and-wife issue, or something deeper?

"There is nothing wrong with Clarence," Sarah said with an edge to her voice.

"I didn't say there was. I was just pointing out that he had different... priorities. You wouldn't have given him a second look before Mandy started dating him."

"I don't give other men a second look," Sarah said with heat.

Josephine could almost hear Thomas grinding his teeth. "What are you saying?" he asked.

"I'm not saying anything," Sarah muttered.

The Kellys looked up to see Josephine and Blasko watching them. They both blushed.

"Sorry. This murder has shaken us up. Can we just not talk about the Ericksons?" Thomas said.

The rest of the evening passed awkwardly with the central topic on everyone's mind having been declared off limits. After another hour, the Kellys finally went home, assuring Josephine they'd had a good time and should do it again soon. Josephine promised they would. No one was being honest.

"I sensed a little tension there," Josephine said as she closed the door behind them.

Blasko chuckled darkly. "More than a little. I wish we'd seen them before the murder. How much of the current attitude between them stems from recent events?"

Josephine shrugged. "She sure seemed jealous of Amanda."

"I don't remember there being any distance between Clarence and Amanda yesterday."

"Maybe Clarence doesn't know."

"Or maybe there isn't anything to know. Your sex has a tendency to see infidelities everywhere," Blasko said haughtily.

"Not just my sex, pal," Josephine shot back.

"True. I've met men who could be jealous of a tree," Blasko agreed.

"Jealousy has certainly led to murder before. Though it

wouldn't make much sense to kill Mr. Erickson."

"And it couldn't be an error. You don't mistake an older man for a middle-aged woman when you're attacking them at close range with a blunt object."

"True." Josephine sighed. "So did our evening of awkward moments get us anywhere?"

"We have more information about the relationships surrounding the murder, which should help us going forward."

"You're really serious about solving this, aren't you?"

"Why are you surprised?" Blasko looked at her with arched eyebrows.

"I don't understand why you care," Josephine said.

Blasko shrugged. "I don't like having a killer stalking around my home."

"Home?"

"I could make a joke about home being where the coffin is." A faint smile crossed his lips.

"Please." Josephine rolled her eyes.

"Obviously, I have secrets to keep. It's better not to have unsolved murders across the street."

"And, unfortunately, your secrets have become my secrets."

"I appreciate you asking the Kellys to dinner, but you don't have to help with this… investigation anymore."

"Didn't I just admit we share some of the same secrets? Besides, I've always had a problem with my curiosity. That's how I got stuck with you."

"Fine."

"So what's the next step, Holmes?"

"I want to know more about Clarence and Amanda," he said, ignoring the reference.

"Don't forget Carrie and Lucy."

"Lucy is a curiosity."

"You don't think she could be involved?"

"I don't know what I think of her."

"She's going to inherit the estate."

"True. And there *was* some tension between her and Mr. Erickson." Blasko went on to tell her about the argument Matthew had described, being intentionally vague about where he'd heard the story.

"I can see that. Erickson was pretty miserly while she is a bit of flash. Not sure what he expected as a rich widower getting married. You're bound to attract the gold diggers. I say that, but they both seemed content with the arrangement. The real question is what's going on with Amanda's and Clarence's marriage."

"If I could be out during the day, I'd take your car into Clarence's garage. That would give me a chance to talk with him."

"Do you even know how to drive?"

"No, and that's not the point," Blasko snapped, slightly embarrassed that he lacked the skill to drive a car. It hadn't escaped his notice that almost everyone drove in this country, with only a few horse-drawn wagons still out on the streets. It was nothing like his home in the mountains where the cart still ruled.

"The viewing is tomorrow night. We can go after dark," Josephine suggested.

"Yes! An excellent opportunity to observe them with the corpse present." Blasko sounded positively giddy at the prospect.

"You know how wrong that is, don't you?"

"Admit it. You're excited too," he said, moving in closer to her.

Josephine looked into his eyes. *Is there a soul there?* she asked herself.

"I think excited would be a bit of an exaggeration. But I do believe you're right. Something is going on in that house, and I'd like to know who's involved."

Blasko reached out and took her shoulders in both his hands. For a moment, Josephine thought he was going to embrace her, and she had no idea how she would react. Instead, he patted her upper arms awkwardly.

"Well, enough of that for the moment. I'm going to go out for a while," he said, turning away.

"What do you do when you go out at night?" she asked his back.

"Nothing. See the town. Feel the fresh air. Get a little exercise," he answered as he took his hat and coat from the rack by the door.

"Fresh air and exercise. That makes you sound… normal," Josephine said with an edge to her voice. Josephine didn't understand her own reaction. Was she angry because he'd never invited her to join him on one of his walks, or was she suspicious of what he was doing all night long?

Blasko turned and stared at her. "You think I'm some sort of monster? You think I don't need a little normalcy? I'll remind you that it was you coming into my home that led to my involvement in your *normal* life." His eyes had hardened into black points.

"Oh, let's not go over that again," she said, and then couldn't stop herself from rehashing the old argument. "I came into your… castle looking for shelter. After your bodyguard killed my companion, I might add. And what did you do? You attacked me."

"Attacked? Darling, if I'd attacked you, you'd be… Well, you wouldn't be standing here berating me," Blasko said indignantly.

"You tried to chew my head off! You only stopped because I bit you!" Josephine couldn't believe he had the gall to suggest otherwise.

Blasko waved his hand as though swatting the suggestion away. "None of that matters now. What is done is done."

"You drive me crazy. You know that?" Josephine said. "Go on. Go on your walk."

"I do not need your permission," he said, turning his back and walking out the door.

"That man is crazy."

Josephine jumped a little, turning to see Grace standing in the doorway to the kitchen.

"He's going to kill us all in our beds. I done tol' you that."

"He's irritating, but he's not crazy."

A quick eye roll made Grace's opinion very clear. "I've finished up the dishes."

"Thank you," Josephine said, meaning as much for staying with her as for the dishes.

Grace hung her apron behind the kitchen door. "I'm goin' up to bed now," she said, walking past Josephine. "But don't think I'm not lockin' my door and puttin' a chair under the knob."

CHAPTER THIRTEEN

Blasko walked out into the cool night air, glad that the heat and humidity of a southern Alabama summer were behind them. Shaking off the frustration of his conversation with Josephine, he set off with a purpose. After talking with the Kellys, he was interested to see the cotton warehouses Thomas owned. He didn't know exactly what he was looking for, but he knew he needed more information about the people in Samuel Erickson's circle of acquaintances.

Unfortunately, Cotton Dock was several miles outside the Sumter city limits. He'd need some transportation. Stealing a horse didn't seem practical. *Why haven't I bought a horse?* he wondered. *Because I'd need to build a stable, that's why.* The town didn't have a working livery anymore and the Nicolsons had long ago turned their carriage house into a garage for their automobile.

In need of help, Blasko found Matthew sitting in a dark corner of the cemetery.

"I used to come here and drink. Made me feel better being with my family." Matthew nodded toward a couple of small headstones. "My mother and father. Mom died while I was overseas and Dad died of the Spanish flu two months after I got home. For all I know, I might have brought it with me. Live with that for a while. And now I can't even drink," he said morosely. "Don't think you did me any favors."

"Say the word and you can get lost in a bottle again," Blasko responded dryly.

Matthew looked up, trying to focus on Blasko's face in the faint glow of the half moon. He opened his mouth, willing himself to say yes, but nothing came out.

"If you are done feeling sorry for yourself, I need a ride."

Matthew chuckled. "You need a ride? What do you think I can do about that?"

"I think you can borrow a car and drive me where I want to go."

"You're a piece of work, you are. I haven't had a friend who'd lend me a car in ten years."

Blasko thought about this for a moment. "Fine, follow me."

"I'm not going…" Matthew began, but Blasko was already headed back in the direction he'd come. "Damn it!" Matthew got up and followed the retreating figure out of the cemetery.

They arrived back at Josephine's house to find that most of the lights were off.

"Wait by the garage," Blasko told Matthew, who shrugged and wandered off toward the back of the house.

Blasko took the stairs to the second floor two at a time. He rapped on Josephine's door, hearing the sound of Fats Waller singing "Ain't Misbehavin'" coming from the radio.

"Who is it?" Josephine's voice asked from the other side of the large oak door.

Blasko thought about yelling back his name, but he hated being on the wrong side of a door. Instead, he turned the knob and walked into the room, only to find it empty.

"Who's out there?" Josephine called from the bathroom.

"It's Blasko," he answered, striding across the room and opening the door to the bathroom.

"What are you doing? I'm taking a bath!" she shouted at

him, sinking farther into the water even as she grabbed for the towel draped over the radiator.

"Don't bother to get up."

"I wasn't going to. We've had these discussions before. You can't just barge into my private space without waiting for permission," Josephine scolded him.

Blasko waved his hand dismissively. "Yes, yes, very sorry," he said without an ounce of sincerity. "I need to take the car."

"Wait one minute!" Josephine desperately wanted to stand up so she could confront him, but there was no way she could without leaving herself in a highly vulnerable state. Instead, she settled for fighting him with logic. "We just discussed this. You… can't… drive!"

"I have someone to drive me," he said, turning to leave as if that could be her only objection.

"Who? You don't… You don't have any friends," Josephine stammered. "Hey!" she yelled to his retreating back and was answered by the slam of her bedroom door.

Josephine sighed and sank back into the warm water. "Fine. Take it. What the hell."

"Where are we going?" Matthew asked as Blasko opened the garage doors.

"For a ride in the country," Blasko told him. He pulled the cord for the electric light, revealing a large, burgundy four-door sedan.

"A Chevrolet," Matthew said admiringly. "'32. Nice. I saw Mr. Nicolson driving this beauty once."

Blasko handed him the key.

"Wowsers. I'll pull it out," Matthew said, wanting to drive the car more than he'd wanted anything other than a bourbon bottle in a decade.

Once the car had eased out of the garage, Blasko gingerly got into the passenger seat.

"You're going to have to tell me which way to go,"

Matthew said, not sounding like he cared. He eased up on the clutch and the big car rolled down the driveway.

"We're going to Cotton Dock," Blasko said, his tone nervous.

"Cotton Dock? At this hour? Why the hell?" Matthew said, putting on the brakes.

"Please, just drive," Blasko said, reaching out and bracing himself against the wood-and-metal dashboard.

"Whatever," Matthew said philosophically. He eased the car out of the driveway, gaining confidence until he was cruising comfortably. "Man, I haven't driven a car in years!" he exclaimed over the wind blowing through the open window. "I forgot how much I loved it."

"I'm not loving it. Slow down," Blasko growled.

"That's because you're not driving," Matthew said, speeding up a little. "I'll teach you sometime."

The road was bumpy and the headlights cast their glow only fifty feet in front of the rocking automobile. It took them almost half an hour to cover the seven miles down to the river and the little settlement of Cotton Dock.

"What's over there?" Blasko asked Matthew, pointing at a building off to the right. There were several cars parked out front and a mule hitched to a post around the side.

"That's the Dock. A juke joint."

"What?"

"A place for the blacks who live down here and work in the warehouses. They got crazy music and, as long as you know the right signals, you can get some hooch."

"Why doesn't the sheriff bust it up?"

"There's a boy up on the roof. If he sees the law coming, he pulls a string that rings a bell inside and all the sweet grain gets poured out on the floor."

"You been in there?"

"Oh, yeah. Anywhere in the county you can get a drink, I've been there."

They passed the Dock and were soon driving by several rows of shotgun shacks.

"Those are the houses where the workers live. Thomas Kelly owns some of them too. He rents them to the workers."

"Serfs."

"What?"

"What do you call them... tenant farmers? They work for the man that owns the land."

"'Bout right. He also runs a small store down here where they can buy stuff on credit. Might as well be slaves. The warehouses are right up here on the last bluff before the river."

"Pull over before we get there," Blasko said.

The main road paralleled the railroad tracks. Matthew turned onto a dirt road that crossed the tracks, then pulled off on the other side under a group of large live oak trees.

"The warehouses are about a hundred feet down the road. There are buildings on both sides of the road and the tracks. Oh, yeah, there's also a loading dock by the tracks."

"Wait here," Blasko said.

"No problem." Matthew settled back in his seat.

Blasko got out and walked toward the warehouses. The night was alive with the sounds of frogs and crickets. Off in the distance, a screech owl gave its trilling call. Blasko's ears picked up every sound. Mixed in with the noise of the insects, amphibians and birds was another sound that came from the cotton warehouse on the left side of the road. He stopped and listened more intently for a moment. Once he was sure of what he was hearing, he continued on.

Blasko could see a sign pointing to the office as he walked closer. His eyes picked out the soft glow of a cigarette coming from inside a car parked beside the office. Just then, the car engine roared to life and the vehicle came bumping up out of the dirt parking lot. Blasko just had time to move back into the bushes to avoid being seen. As the car drove past, he thought he recognized the square-jawed face of Thomas Kelly. A woman was in the passenger seat, but Blasko couldn't see her face well enough to tell if it was

Sarah or not.

He continued down to the warehouse, more cautious now in case anyone else was there. But as he circled the buildings, he didn't see any other cars or people. Finally, having snooped around the buildings to his satisfaction, he headed back to the car.

"Find anything?"

"There was a car parked down there."

"Okay. So…?"

"They left in a hurry. Curious."

"What's that?"

"I could hear them as I approached. What I heard was… distinctive. Why would someone park their car out here and…Well… Do…" Blasko stumbled to find the right words.

"Do what? Oh, you're a real bluenose. You mean they were puttin' the boots to it."

"Yes, I suppose they were… Right. Why here?"

"Ha, 'cause they can't do it anywhere else."

"I think it was Kelly."

"Thomas Kelly? Now that's interesting. I think you can take it to the bank that the woman wasn't his wife."

"I didn't get a good look at her. But I take your point. It sounded like they were… doing it in the car."

"Yeah, quick and dirty. Didn't want to go in the office or couldn't wait."

"We can go home now."

"The hell you say. I ain't goin' to be your chauffer all the time. You can't be out in the sun, right?"

"No, as I've told you, I'm—"

"Allergic. Yeah, I got that. Come on. We still have plenty of time." Matthew got out and made Blasko switch places with him.

Matthew explained all the intricacies of the clutch, shifter, brake and gas pedal, slowly and carefully. "Think you got it?"

"I understand the principle," Blasko said.

"That's as good as it gets without the engine running. Go

on. Turn the switch and press the button."

Blasko did as instructed and the engine started anemically.

"Yeah, give it a little gas."

Ten minutes later, they were creeping slowly down the road. It had been a ragged start, with Blasko frequently panicking when the car would lurch forward from too much gas and then overcompensating with too much brake.

"I think I've got this," Blasko said, eventually speeding up. The car bumped and jostled down the road. "I see why you like driving."

Matthew just nodded, still nursing an elbow that had banged into the dash more than once and wondering what sort of monster he might have created.

All seemed to go well until they approached a turn in town. Blasko went too wide, bounced over a curb and hit a lamppost.

"It's not too bad," Matthew said, examining the damage to the car.

"They shouldn't put the lampposts that close to the street."

"Yeah, that's the problem," Matthew said dryly.

"A trip to Clarence's garage might be in order," Blasko said contemplatively.

CHAPTER FOURTEEN

Josephine saw the note from Blasko when she got up. "I can't believe that man," she grumbled.

"I seen that," Grace said, shaking her head. "What's that fool doing drivin' around? Can he even do that?"

"The state is thinking about passing a law that would require all drivers to have a license. But they haven't done it yet."

"Another thing poor people goin' to have to pay for," Grace said.

Josephine didn't bother to ask her which was worse: having unqualified drivers or charging people for a license.

After breakfast, Josephine looked again at the note telling her of the damage to the car. Now that she was fully awake, she understood the significance of Blasko telling her to keep an eye out when she took the car to Clarence's garage to get it fixed. A little thrill went through her at the thought of doing some detective work. *I'm getting as crazy as he is*, she told herself.

An hour later, Josephine pulled up in front of the garage. The original part of the building was a very small store with a couple of gas pumps out front. A large addition had been built after Clarence had taken over the business. Everyone knew it had been old man Erickson's money that had built it. It would have been more fodder for gossip if Clarence hadn't been a good mechanic and a hard worker.

Josephine parked in front of an empty bay. A large man with a chocolate complexion and wearing greasy grey overalls walked quickly over to the car. He put his fingers up to his cap in greeting.

"Howdy, Miss Josephine. If you need gas, just pull up to the pumps. Or I can do it for you."

Josephine recognized the man. He was a cousin of Jerome, her yardman, and had come over to help Jerome a few times with large jobs.

"It's Mills, right?"

"Yes, ma'am."

Josephine got out and showed Mills the damage to the front of the car.

"Mr. Clarence ain't here today. He and Mrs. Erickson are too broken up over his daddy's… you know." He couldn't bring himself to say the word "murder."

"Of course," Josephine said, feeling disappointed.

"You could come by next week. I expect he'll be back then. They going to bury Mr. Erickson this weekend."

"Did Mr. Erickson come by here often?" Josephine realized that Mills might be a good source of information.

"Nah, not often. Mr. Clarence didn't like it when he did." Mills looked around, making sure no one was listening. "When Mr. Erickson come around, Mr. Clarence would be yelling and cursing up a storm the rest of the day."

"They didn't get along?"

"I wouldn't say that. I just don't think Mr. Clarence liked his daddy looking over his shoulder. Mr. Erickson would always tell him what he was doing wrong."

"Like what?"

"Oh, prices were too low or too high. New stuff needed to be out front where it could be seen. How Mr. Clarence shouldn't give anyone credit. Stuff like that. Mr. Clarence didn't mind as much if Mrs. Erickson was along."

"His stepmother?"

"That's right. Both Mr. Clarence and Mr. Erickson were a little better when she was around."

"What about Amanda?"

"I don't know anything about that," Mills said quickly.

"I just meant did she come by often?" Josephine understood his nervousness. Black men weren't supposed to notice the comings and goings of white women.

"Nah, I don't think she liked the garage much. Always worried she was going to get dirty. She'd stand right in the middle away from everything."

"Was Clarence in a good mood after his wife would come by?" Josephine asked, knowing that she was probably pushing the bounds of conversation beyond common gossip and into the realm of nosiness.

"Guess he decided to come in after all," Mills said suddenly, looking past Josephine to where a striking red Packard roadster convertible was pulling up to the garage.

Clarence was behind the wheel. He looked over at Josephine with an expression that might have conveyed interest or suspicion. Josephine wasn't sure. She waved to him as Mills walked over to the car.

Clarence and Mills spoke for a moment in voices too low for her to hear. *If I'm going to be a detective, then I'm going to have to learn to read lips*, Josephine told herself, smiling inwardly at the thought of herself as a detective.

"Hello, Josephine. Mills says you've got a damaged fender," Clarence said, walking over to her.

"I don't want to bother you. You should be with your family."

"I'll just take a quick look and give you an estimate. But you're right. I need to get back to the house. I just wanted to make sure that Mills didn't need anything." Clarence walked around the vehicle, looking it over. "Nice car. Your father asked me for a recommendation when he was thinking about buying it."

"He didn't know a thing about cars. I'm sure he

appreciated your advice." Josephine watched him closely. "Have you heard anything from Sheriff Logan?"

Clarence looked up at her with narrowed eyes. "He told me that you all shouldn't have been asking questions and looking in the bedroom the other night."

Josephine felt her cheeks grow warm. "I know we were overstepping our bounds a bit. But the baron really does have experience in… these areas. He thought he could help."

"He's a strange duck," Clarence said flatly.

"Yes, he is that." Josephine couldn't help but agree.

Clarence seemed surprised at her comment, his lips turning up in a small smile. "I'll be able to clean this up for, say, about nine dollars," he said, looking at the damaged car.

"How's business been?" Josephine asked him. This would have seemed like an odd question coming from most women, but as she had a controlling interest in the bank, folks tended to accept her interest in business.

"Oh, you know. Like everyone else, we take a few more chickens or bushels of corn in trade than we did before the crash, but it's always been hardscrabble around here. My grandfather had a cotton farm that got wiped out by the boll weevil."

"'Hard times come again no more,'" Josephine quoted.

"Exactly." Clarence paused for a minute and then added, "Sheriff hasn't got any leads. They chased down a bunch of hobos, but nothing came of it. I got to talk to Mills and then get back to the house. Bring the car in next week." Clarence tipped his hat to her, then headed over to where Mills was taking the tire off of an old Model A.

A black car with a gold star on the door was parked in front of her house when Josephine pulled into the driveway. Deputy Bobby Tucker was waiting for her at the front door.

"Howdy," Bobby said.

"Have you been waiting long?"

"No. I came by and Grace said you were out. When I turned around to leave, I saw you pulling into the driveway."

He paused.

"And?"

"I want to talk to you." He seemed unsure how to continue.

"Well, I'm here," Josephine said, a little exasperated. She'd been avoiding Bobby since she'd gotten back from Europe. She didn't want to invite him inside, knowing how much harder it would be to end the conversation if he was ensconced in the house.

"Why are you sticking your nose into this murder?" he blurted out. "This isn't really any of your business."

"That's not fair. Mr. Erickson was my neighbor. I can see his house from here," she said, pointing at it. "That murder was almost literally in my front yard."

"It's that freak you have living here," Bobby grumbled.

"How dare you come here and pass judgment on a guest in my house?" To herself, Josephine had to admit that, yes, Blasko was a bit of a freak. But that wasn't any of Bobby Tucker's damn business.

"Guest?! He's been here six months. I tell you, Josie, people are talking."

"I couldn't care less what people are saying behind my back. If they have a problem with me or my friends, they should come right out and say it to my face."

"And how are they going to do that? You control the only bank in town. Most of the folks around here owe money to the bank one way or the other. All of the farms need loans to plant every year." Bobby stopped. Having stumbled into this argument, he was surprised to be verbalizing thoughts that had previously been just nebulous ideas in his head. For the first time, he was seeing how important Josephine had become in the community.

"That's stupid. The bank is run by a board, and what we do or don't do is determined by rules set up by my father and other good men." She fought back the urge to say: *And if they're really worried about their money, then they shouldn't make me mad.* Josephine sighed and asked, "Why are you here,

Bobby?"

"You've been avoiding me ever since you got back."

"And if I have, then what do you think that means?" Josephine was beyond irritated. She liked Bobby and she really didn't want to hurt his feelings, but she didn't like having to explain herself.

"I don't know," he said with an expression that reminded her of a lost puppy. "I thought we were… I don't know… more than friends."

"We're friends. I don't know about anything more than that. I've known you since grade school, but…"

"You aren't even treating me like a friend. Now you admit you've been avoiding me. Is that fair?"

"Damn it! Okay, sit down," Josephine said, indicating one of the wicker chairs on the porch. Out of the corner of her eye, she saw motion at the window and turned to see Grace pulling her head back quickly behind the drapes.

Bobby sat down. The holster on his hip made it awkward for him to get comfortable in the small chair.

Josephine sat down across from him. "With my father dying and the trip overseas, I've just been spending the last few months trying to settle back into a routine." She really didn't want to discuss Blasko and hoped to avoid bringing him up again.

Bobby had other ideas. "I just don't understand who this baron guy is. You said he was some sort of distant relative, but… I don't know. Why did you bring him home?"

"What business is that of yours?"

"You said we were friends. Shouldn't a friend be concerned if he sees a friend getting involved in something that maybe that friend shouldn't be involved in?" Bobby blurted out.

Josephine found it hard to stay angry in the face of his obvious sincerity and hangdog expression. "It's a long story. He needs to be here right now. You just have to take my word for that."

"Why is he so interested in this murder?"

"For the same reason I am. It happened across the street. Have you all been making any progress in solving it?" she threw at him to change the subject.

"No. The sheriff got it in his head that it had to be a stranger and we've been chasing bogeymen for the last few days. But I tell you, Logan's going to have to come around to the idea that it's someone closer to home. When he does, your friend could find himself in the crosshairs."

"What are you talking about?"

"We've already gotten a call claiming that he could be involved. I'll just leave it at that." Bobby's eyes hardened.

"What busybody was that?" Josephine asked, already suspecting the nosy Evie.

"Doesn't matter who it is. Sheriff Logan is eventually going to give up on his hobo theory and, when he does, his next choice is going to be people who arrived in town during the last year. And your puffed-up baron is going to be right at the top of the list."

"Exactly. So now you understand why we're interested in finding the killer," Josephine said, feeling vindicated.

"I hear what you're selling, but I'm not buying it. What y'all are doing just draws more attention to the pair of you."

"You're accusing me now?"

"No, you know better than that. I just mean you aren't making friends with the sheriff by interfering."

"Who do you think killed him?" Josephine tried again to divert the conversation. Besides, she was curious about Bobby's opinion. Bobby was a bit of a teddy bear, but he wasn't stupid and he took his job seriously.

"I've hardly had time to think about it, chasing down every hobo in southern Alabama and Georgia. But I think we need to look at Erickson's enemies. The man had a lot of them."

"What about the family?" Josephine asked.

Bobby's face was conflicted and Josephine understood why. The idea that one of Erickson's family chose to bludgeon him to death seemed too brutal.

"Maybe," Bobby finally said. "But I'm telling you, the sheriff is going to be most interested in someone like your baron. Someone who hasn't been in town that long and who insists on hanging around the investigation."

"Maybe you have a point." Knowing she'd gotten all the information she could on the murder investigation, and afraid that Bobby would try to turn the conversation back to their relationship, Josephine stood up quickly. "Bobby, I appreciate you stopping by, but I need to go in now. I really should see what Grace is up to." She thought she heard a small *huff* from the other side of the window.

Bobby stood reluctantly. "Okay. But we need to talk… about us," he said, looking embarrassed.

"We will. Later." *If I can't avoid it*, Josephine thought.

CHAPTER FIFTEEN

After spending all of Friday fretting about whether taking Blasko to the viewing of Erickson's body was a good idea, the time had arrived. Josephine knocked on his door, which flew open immediately.

"Come in." Blasko was still wearing his robe. "It came to me that I had no idea what to wear."

"A black suit is fine," Josephine said, amused at Blasko's sudden interest in fitting in.

"Ahhh. Customs vary in the Carpathians. White is the color of mourning for some, while for others it is black. In some areas, the women wear a dark dress with a white veil."

"Do you have viewings?" Josephine asked, curious about the customs of her ancestors.

"There are vigils in the home of the deceased. The men make the coffin and other objects for the funeral while the women clean and sit with the body. The mirrors are covered, clocks are stopped and the windows are closed."

"Hmmm… We also drape the mirrors and stop the clocks," Josephine said. "Which brings up a question I've wanted to ask you. Why are you afraid of mirrors?"

"What do you mean?" Blasko tried to sound nonchalant.

"I've seen you avert your eyes every time you pass a

mirror. And you don't have a single mirror down here. Why?"

His answer was so long in coming that Josephine thought he was choosing to ignore her. But after a moment he averted his eyes and, his tone subdued, said, "I am... unnatural... When I look in a mirror I see myself as if I have been dead and buried for hundreds of years. At first I worried that others could see me like this, but in time I realized only I could see the face of my true destiny. A constant reminder that my existence is an abomination in the eyes of God."

Josephine tried to look him in the eyes, but he wouldn't meet her gaze. "You're imagining it," she said with more assurance than she felt.

"Ha, no," was all he said. Blasko sat down in a chair, seeming to draw inside himself as she watched.

Josephine could understand regrets. She had her share. She wondered what it must be like to have hundreds of years of regrets.

"Maybe it's a reminder that your extended existence is a gift that shouldn't be wasted," she said at last.

He raised his eyes, his expression curious. "Perhaps."

"Come on, we have a murderer to catch. You need to get dressed," she urged.

Blasko came over to her and touched her cheek. "Trust me. We *will* find this killer."

Josephine stood still, frozen at his touch. She tried to blink, but could not look away from his penetrating gaze. She felt herself flush. Then, as quickly as the moment had started, it ended and Blasko backed away.

Trying to recover, Josephine heard that annoying squeaking again. She looked up and saw movement in the shadows near the ceiling, but she still couldn't identify the source of the irritating noise.

"Fine, I'll get dressed now," Blasko said, making an obvious effort to rush Josephine out the door.

"What *is* that?" Josephine asked, pointing toward the

rafters.

"Nothing, I'm sure." Blasko's accent had become more pronounced. Josephine had learned early on in their relationship that the more nervous he got, the harder his English was to understand.

Still looking at the ceiling, Josephine suddenly jumped back. "What the hell! That's a bat!"

She was pointing at Vasile, who took this as his cue to flutter down and land on Blasko's shoulder. For his part, Blasko tried to pretend he didn't see the animal as it shuffled in closer to his neck.

Josephine stood staring at them both, her mouth hanging open.

"His name is Vasile," Blasko finally said.

"He... ah... has a name?" Josephine stammered.

"He is very friendly. I found him and rescued him."

"I'm sorry, but we take in dogs and cats in this country, not... not bats." Strangely, Josephine realized she was more stunned by the revelation that Blasko had a pet bat than by any of his other oddities.

"I took a liking to bats many years ago," Blasko said, reaching up and scratching Vasile, who spread his wings appreciatively.

"I know you're... a... little... I mean, a *lot* different than other people... but bats?" Josephine cocked her head, squinting at the animal as she tried to decide if the bat was the ugliest thing she'd ever seen or if, maybe, it was kind of... possibly... cute.

"It's a long story." Blasko seemed embarrassed.

"This I have to hear."

"Do you really want me to tell you?"

He sounded almost child-like. His tone had an oddly humble quality that she'd never heard from him. It made Josephine soften her own attitude. "Yes." And she added, "Please."

Blasko stroked Vasile as he spoke. "I was nine years old. Of course, this was long before I was subject to my...

condition. In those days, the castle was smaller and alive with my family and the villagers who lived under its protection. It was two weeks before All Saints Day and the annual celebrations of the harvest. My father and most of the men had ridden out on the Great Hunt, as they did almost every year. The hunt would last for over a week and, when they returned, they would bring venison, fowl and game. Enough to feed everyone at the festival several times over.

"But this year, after they had been gone two days, there came a great thunder up the pass. We never learned whether a traitor in our midst had informed our enemies that most of the men were gone, or if they had found out on their own. Either way, a horde of Turkish cavalry attacked the castle. All males over the age of ten were slaughtered, and most of the women were killed or raped. Even though I was younger than ten, I would have been killed anyway because of my lineage if they had found me, but a servant girl rushed me up the winding stone steps in one of the castle's older towers. The structure was in disrepair and not used anymore. The room at the top had a wooden ceiling. By climbing up through the fireplace chimney, I was able to get into the small space between the ceiling and stone roof of the turret.

"I hid up there for weeks. The servant girl would sneak me table scraps. The roof leaked and provided me with rainwater to drink. I had food and water, but no one to talk to, no one to whom I could confide my fears. As I tried not to think about the fate of my family or the future that might await me, the only companionship I had were the bats that nested in the stone crevices of the tower. For many days I talked to the bats and, in time, they accepted me. Together, we listened for weeks as my father and his men fought to retake the castle. When they were finally victorious, I climbed down from the tower and brought with me a bat who had become especially acclimated to my presence. I knew that my new friend made my father and surviving family and friends feel uncomfortable, but knowing what I had gone through during the battle, they indulged my small... quirk."

Vasile had climbed onto Blasko's hand and he held the creature out slowly to Josephine.

"I hear they eat a lot of mosquitoes," was all Josephine could think to say about the big-eared critter.

"You can pet him," Blasko encouraged.

"Thanks," Josephine said with an ironic edge to her voice as she screwed up her courage to pet the leather-bound creature. Finally, she extended her hand and lightly touched Vasile on his fuzzy back. He squeaked and stretched. Josephine backed away.

"I think that's enough interaction for today," she said. "You should know that if Grace sees that... er... him, she won't stop screaming until you're both out of the house."

Blasko gave a slight bow in acknowledgment of this truth.

"Okay, put your friend down and go get dressed," Josephine said in a small voice and headed back up the stairs. "I'll meet you in the parlor."

As she took her mourning dress out of the wardrobe, Josephine was hit with a sudden flood of emotion. Her father's sickness and death came back to her in a fresh wave of unexpected pain. She had to steady herself for a moment before taking a deep breath and putting the dress on. Lately, she'd felt like she was in an emotional windstorm. *I can't let all the craziness around me get the best of me*, she told herself.

By the time Josephine entered the parlor, Blasko was there waiting for her, dressed immaculately in a black silk suit and tie.

"Dapper as always," she complimented him.

"Should you look... dapper for a viewing?"

"Honestly, as long as it's not for a child, a funeral is more of a social event in Alabama."

"Even if the person was murdered?" Blasko asked, raising his eyebrows.

"I wouldn't know. This is my first viewing for a murder victim. But if I had to guess, I'd say there'll be more people there sightseeing than mourning."

"It would be the same anywhere in the world."

Blasko held out his arm to her. They had almost reached the door when Grace abruptly appeared in the hallway.

"Ain't this cozy," she huffed. "You two are just gonna get yourselves in trouble. That's what Mr. Tucker told you." Grace seemed to have forgotten she'd learned this last bit of information by eavesdropping.

"Your concern is duly noted. Thank you," Josephine said with more than a little sarcasm.

"Suit yourselves," Grace said, wiping her hands of the matter.

"That woman is taking on the role of a harpy in our little Greek tragedy," Blasko observed as they walked down the porch stairs.

"She doesn't mean any harm. You have to realize that all of this is stressful for her too," Josephine told him.

The door of the Erickson house was being manned by a properly solemn cousin of the family whose name escaped Josephine. He thanked them for coming and asked them to sign the guest book. Inside, the house was full, even though the viewing had started an hour ago. Many folks had stayed to talk with friends they seldom saw or had time to socialize with. Though few would have admitted it, most were titillated at being in close proximity to a crime that was being reported in papers as far away as Atlanta and New Orleans.

The first person Josephine saw was Bobby Tucker, who was dressed in an old, ill-fitting black suit. He nodded to her and gave Blasko a not-so-veiled glare.

"We should steer clear of him," she whispered to Blasko.

"Baron," a voice said from behind them. They both turned and saw Thomas Kelly, looking dark and brooding in a black pinstriped suit. "Josephine."

"Mr. Kelly," Blasko said, watching him closely for any sign that Kelly might have been aware Blasko had seen him with another woman. Heard him with another woman would be more accurate, but Blasko didn't feel the need to split hairs.

"I told you to call me Thomas."

"Have you seen Clarence and Amanda?" Josephine asked, trying not to make eye contact. Blasko had told her what Kelly had been doing at the warehouse. She couldn't get the image of him cheating on his wife out of her head.

"Yes, I think they're out back. Amanda was pretty upset."

"Poor thing," Josephine said. "I should go find her."

Thomas looked like he wanted to say something, but stopped himself.

Josephine left Blasko with Thomas, figuring it was safe enough as they'd already gotten to know each other, and headed off in search of Amanda. She looked in the kitchen, but didn't see anyone other than a couple of maids who looked like they'd rather be somewhere else.

As she passed the library, she could hear the faint sound of voices coming from a porch off the side of the house. She could just see two figures standing in the dark by the porch railing. Without turning on the light, Josephine crept closer to the door. When she was a few feet away, she could finally make out some of what they were saying.

Amanda and Clarence were having a heated discussion, but they were doing it in half whispers that obscured many of their words.

"I'm tired of it," Josephine heard Clarence say.

"You're being ridiculous. I'm not…"

"I know what… You don't."

Amanda's response was equally garbled. "Nonsense… I wouldn't… you… unnatural."

"…dare you? I'm not… Now… move out…"

"…get through this…"

"I swear…" Clarence growled.

"…can't stand it…"

Josephine wished she could ask them to speak up. She started to move closer when suddenly they stopped talking and turned toward the door. Josephine had to run on her toes to get out of the room quickly and quietly enough not to get caught.

She found Blasko in a corner of the parlor talking with Jerry Connelly, the mortician. She pulled him away from their deep discussion regarding the virtues of the different types of wood used in coffin construction.

"I just caught Clarence and Amanda arguing," she told him.

"About what?"

"I couldn't make it out very well. They both seemed equally angry. Like they were accusing each other of something."

"Interesting. I've been observing the daughter, Carrie. Not very social. Connelly was telling me how difficult she's been over the funeral arrangements. Arguing over everything and trying to talk him down on every cost."

"Can't say I'm surprised. She's certainly her father's daughter. Though it's strange that Lucy wasn't the one to make the arrangements."

"Connelly said that every time Lucy started to speak, Carrie would shut her down."

They both turned to look at the pair standing by the coffin. Lucy seemed oddly animated by the tragedy, while Carrie stood straight and stiff, looking uncomfortable whenever anyone talked to her. Not once did they see her try to comfort her stepmother.

"That's one cold fish," Josephine said. "I'm going over to give my condolences."

Blasko followed her.

"I'm so sorry for your loss," Josephine told Carrie.

"Thank you," Carrie replied, looking past Josephine and barely nodding at Blasko. He could hear her heart beating fast. She was clearly under emotional pressure.

"Lucy, this must be horrible for you," Josephine said.

"It's such a tragedy. Why? I keep asking myself, why did it happen?" Lucy looked down at her husband's coffin, placing her hand on the lid.

"If there is anything I can do, just let me know,"

Josephine said, looking at both women before walking passed the closed coffin.

For a while, Blasko and Josephine stood at the back of the room and watched the mourners and sightseers file by the coffin. Lucy stayed beside the bier and greeted the people, though Carrie had wandered off. At one point, when Amanda and Clarence walked by, all three of them seemed ill at ease. Lucy didn't make eye contact with either of them.

There is something odd going on with this family, Josephine thought. *Is it just the cliché of the disliked stepmother? Or do they suspect each other?*

Blasko and Josephine were heading for the door when Evangeline Anderson walked in. Though she tried, Josephine couldn't see any way to get to the door without passing within speaking distance of her neighbor. Sure enough, the older woman stepped directly into their path and locked eyes with Josephine.

"Terrible, isn't it? It's so hard to see how something like a murder could happen in our own quiet neighborhood. I never would have imagined it six months ago," she said, looking pointedly at Blasko. "How is your allergy, by the way? It must be terrible not being able to go out during the day. If you could, you might have seen the man that murdered Mr. Erickson."

"If you'll excuse us, we were just leaving. I'm sure you'll want to pay your respects to the Ericksons," Josephine said, trying to step around Evangeline. When she did, she almost bumped into Lucy Erickson, who had suddenly appeared at her side.

"Could I talk with you alone for a minute?" Lucy asked. Josephine looked at Evangeline and Blasko. She didn't really want to leave them alone, but she was intrigued by Lucy's request.

"Of course," she finally said, giving Blasko a look meant to stop him from engaging with Evangeline.

She followed Lucy out of the parlor and into the dining room. There was no one else in the room and Lucy sank down into one of the chairs at the table.

"I hope you don't mind me sitting down. These last few days have been very hard on me." The woman's natural good looks showed through, despite the grief she'd been battling since the murder.

"What can I do for you?" Josephine asked, sitting down beside her.

"Well, I appreciate what you and your friend have been trying to do. I... just... Well, I honestly don't know what to say. I guess I'm worried about Carrie. She seems... distracted. Maybe it's just grief or the shock of the murder."

"You think she knows something?"

"I wouldn't go that far. I just think there is something going on that Carrie isn't telling me. I'm truly worried about her."

"Have you said something to the sheriff?"

"That old goat! No. I just wondered if your friend has found out anything? It would be such a relief to know who did this."

"He's keeping his eyes open, but right now we really don't know anything more than anyone else. Are you worried that something might happen to Carrie? Or... well... do you think that she could be involved somehow?" Josephine was trying to be delicate.

Lucy stood up abruptly. "I don't know what I know. There's just this feeling of foreboding. Nonsense, really. Probably natural after someone you love is murdered in your own home. I'm sorry to bother you with it." It was clear that Lucy didn't want to talk anymore.

She started toward the door and Josephine followed her back into the parlor. Before they parted, Josephine touched Lucy's arm. "If you see or hear anything that frightens you, please let me know. Any time, day or night."

"Thank you, Josephine. You've always been a good neighbor," Lucy said, her eyes resting on Carrie, who was back beside the coffin.

Josephine didn't see Blasko in the parlor. She finally

found him in the front yard, standing back to gaze at the house. He'd had to go outside to escape the persistent and odious Anderson woman. In front of them, the windows of the house glowed with a festive light that was in stark contrast to the solemn ritual taking place inside.

"I'm always fascinated with the places where horrors occur. Often they are such mundane locations until events overtake them. Afterward, they seem burdened by their own history, even as they maintain their pedestrian nature."

"Just looks like a house to me," Josephine said flatly.

"Not in a philosophical mood?" Blasko joked with her. "What did the widow want?"

"That is a good question. At first she seemed to want to unburden herself, but she must have changed her mind because all she did was talk about some vague sense of dread surrounding Carrie."

"Maybe that's all she has." Blasko shrugged. "A feeling."

"Women's intuition? A gut feeling? Maybe." Josephine wasn't sure. "There seemed to be something else going on. Maybe she was scared to say what she knew. Of course, this is just *my* intuition."

"I'd trust your feelings," Blasko said. Josephine wondered if he was referring to more than her thoughts about Lucy,

They walked back to the house, but Blasko did not join her on the porch.

"Going out for another walk?"

"I think so."

"As long as you aren't going for another drive," Josephine said with a laugh.

"I only need a little more practice."

"I'm not sure my car can survive another lesson."

"Good night, Josephine," he said, turning away.

"Goodnight." Something in his eyes made her add, "Be careful."

CHAPTER SIXTEEN

Blasko felt weak. The mental and physical activity of the last few days had left him drained. He hadn't let on to Josephine, but the blood she had acquired for him didn't provide everything he needed. Like a person whose diet doesn't include enough vitamin C, he could survive, but not thrive. He needed fresh blood. He'd resisted the urge for as long as he could, but he couldn't deny it anymore.

He'd known the day would come, so on his nightly walks he'd kept his eyes and ears open. He wouldn't take an innocent and he wouldn't kill. But he would attack, and he had several victims in mind.

He focused his hearing as he approached a house he'd previously made note of. Here all was quiet. No one was home. He turned his attention to another location and his remarkable hearing picked up the sound of voices from almost a block away. The second house was closer to the Erickson home than he was comfortable with, but he would take the chance. No one would die.

Standing in the yard, he heard the smack of flesh against flesh and a cry of pain. Angry curses were followed by desperate pleading. The scene was too familiar—a loving and supplicant woman at the mercy of a cruel and stupid man.

Blasko must have witnessed this same tableau play out thousands of times over the centuries and the unnecessary pain always infuriated him.

A third voice, young and scared, joined the others as a boy begged his father to leave his mother alone. There was another slap. Blasko wanted to barge inside and drag the man from the house, but he knew he had to wait and let the scene play out. The odds were good that the man would storm out; it was just a matter of time.

After minutes that seemed like hours, the back door flew open and the squat, ugly shape of the man emerged into the night. Blasko quickly fell into step behind the staggering, drunken buffoon. He wasn't surprised. They were usually drunk.

Blasko followed the man until he neared a decrepit shed in a small alley. Blasko moved up behind the drunk and reached out, grabbing the man's hair and yanking it backward. Like a Vaudevillian comic routine, the man's feet flew up in front of him. Blasko slammed him hard against the ground, knocking the wind from his lungs.

With a motion that came naturally after centuries of hunting, Blasko sank his teeth deep into the man's throat and drank. With great skill he'd avoided the main artery, choosing lesser vessels to slake his thirst while preserving life. He took as much as he dared before leaving the despicable man alone and lying in his own filth.

His thirst and the means of satisfying it left him feeling unclean. Blasko walked the night, trying to forget that his renewed strength and energy came at the cost of his dignity, if not his soul. It seemed a cruel irony that he had no more knowledge about the afterlife than anyone else. For the better part of a century after his transformation, he had sought answers from philosophy and theology, only to realize that, for him, there were no answers.

Twelve hours later, Blasko was awakened in his coffin by

someone pounding on his door. It must have started before the sun was even below the trees. He rose and shouted for whoever it was to have patience. He found a robe and strode to the door, flinging it open.

"What?" He wasn't surprised to see Josephine. Who else would be waking him up? But he was shocked to see the mix of fear and urgency on her face.

"There's been another killing."

Blasko's first thought was to reassure himself that he'd left the wife-beater alive. Of course, he also knew that things could happen.

"Who and where?" he asked, trying not to sound too paranoid.

Josephine had waited most of the day to talk with Blasko and now the words poured out. "Amanda Erickson. They found her beaten body under some bushes about a block from the house. They've arrested a man they discovered not too far from the body. He was asleep or knocked out or just plain drunk. He had blood all over him. Sheriff Logan says they found the murder weapon close by." Josephine paused to take a breath.

Blasko didn't know where to begin. Who was the man? Were they sure he was involved? Then a thought occurred to him. Could the wife-beater and the man they thought was the killer be one and the same?

"Come in while I get dressed," he said.

Josephine was surprised at Blasko's subdued reaction. She'd expected him to be energized by the news. The events were horrible and shocking, but also fascinating on some level. Besides, it could mean that the killer had been captured. She walked into the parlor and paced back and forth while he dressed.

"How can we find out more information?" Blasko asked, coming out of his bedroom and heading for the stairs.

"I could talk to Bobby," Josephine said reluctantly. "He'd certainly know what's going on. But I'd rather not use that source. There *is* someone else. However, there's a risk."

"Which is?"

"It's Emmett Wolfe. I pointed him out at the viewing. He's the editor of the *Sumter Times*."

"And what's the risk?"

"His curiosity. I've tried very hard not to draw his attention since I've been back. He came by as soon as he heard about you, wanting to know who you are, why you're here, all of that gossip column fodder. I showed you the small article."

"It was rather thin on details," Blasko said dryly. His ego had been a little bruised at the time.

"That was on purpose. You do *not* want him getting interested in your back story. I promise you, he's capable of doing some first-class excavating when he starts digging."

"I see," Blasko muttered, frustrated that his background required secrecy.

"However, the bank holds a decent-size mortgage on the paper. He borrowed quite a large sum to put in a new printing press just before the market crashed and I know he's had a hard time meeting the note."

"So he's not likely to want to get on the wrong side of the person who heads up the bank's board of directors."

"Exactly. I hate using my position, though he's smart enough that I won't have to point it out to him. Of course, that would come into play only if he gets too aggressive in investigating you." Josephine was feeling very Machiavellian.

"I didn't realize what it would mean entering the twentieth century," Blasko said. "I really am sorry for the trouble I'm causing you." He hoped the latest murder and arrest of a suspect wouldn't escalate the trouble.

"Nothing that can't be handled," Josephine said with more confidence than she was feeling. Her life had become a series of risks and she hadn't decided how she felt about that. On one hand, the complications were driving her a bit mad, but on the other she'd never felt so alive. She was pretty sure that time would tell if the rewards were worth the risks.

"Call him," Blasko encouraged.

Josephine hated to use the telephone. She knew that Dolly, the operator, would be listening in. The woman wasn't even subtle about it—half the time Josephine could hear the sound of Dolly smacking gum in the background as she tried to carry on a conversation. At least Dolly was the only one who could eavesdrop. Josephine's father had installed a private line several years ago, figuring the banking business was not something you wanted on a party line.

With a sigh, Josephine picked up the phone. After getting through the pleasantries, Josephine decided on a direct approach with Emmett.

"You know that I live right across the street from the Ericksons, and this horrible business with the murders has me and my household upset. I don't want to bother the sheriff, but I thought maybe you could tell me what's going on." Josephine did her best to sound like a helpless female scared of the events swirling around her.

"I'll be glad to tell you what I know. I just finished the copy for tomorrow. The presses are running as we speak."

"Thank you soooo much."

"I can come over now if you like. Of course, I'd want to have a chance to meet your houseguest. You've been promising me an interview with him for months."

Trust Emmett to use his leverage on her. Josephine took a deep breath. What choice did she have? "That would be fine. I know he'll be delighted to talk with you. Though I'm surprised that, with all the drama going on, you have time for a social column."

"One thing I've learned as a journalist is that life goes on. I'm on my way." He hung up before she could change her mind.

He rapped on the door twenty minutes later. Emmett was thin and balding, with a natural folksiness that encouraged people to relax and want to talk to him. His inquisitive eyes were always scanning for something interesting. As soon as he saw Blasko, Emmett's eyes locked on him.

"This is surely a pleasure," Emmett said, sticking his hand out to Blasko.

The baron took it reluctantly and responded, "The same." In truth, he never trusted anyone who was too anxious to shake hands. He considered the act a formal ceremony to be performed only with someone you've already decided to trust.

"Josephine's been keeping you hidden. Semmes County doesn't get many folks from Europe. As a small-town editor, I live for the unusual. So let's talk about you," he said, sitting down in the parlor. Emmett had learned long ago that once he got a foot in the door, he needed to make sure it wasn't easy for someone to push it back out again.

"Emmett, I'd really like to know what's going on with these murders," Josephine said, keeping up her frightened female act.

Reluctantly, Emmett turned his focus away from Blasko. "Logan thinks he's got his man and I have to say it looks pretty good from what I've seen. The man they've arrested is a nasty character. I've seen a couple reports on him over the years. When he gets drunk he gets mean."

"What's his name?"

"Floyd Hopkins. He drives a truck for the feed store, mostly delivering large orders to farmers," Emmett said. It was clear he wanted to shift the conversation to Blasko.

"You said he'd been in trouble before," Josephine pressed.

"Bar fights, mostly. But the sheriff said they'd been out to his house a few times when the neighbors had called complaining about fights with his wife. Deputy Tucker said that, the last time he went out there, the fight was mostly Hopkins beating up on the wife. Tucker brought him to the station that night, but couldn't hold him since the wife wouldn't press charges."

Blasko, sitting across from Emmett, listened intently. The more he heard about the man, the more concerned he was that they were talking about the same man he'd attacked the night before.

Emmett looked at Blasko again. "Now, the deal is I get to interview the baron in exchange for all this information," he said good-naturedly.

Josephine nodded. "Yes, we'll keep our word. But first, is the sheriff sure this man killed the Ericksons?"

"No. I mean, yes, the sheriff seems sure right now. But he hasn't checked all the facts yet. Hopkins could have an air-tight alibi for Mr. Erickson's murder. The way it stands now, the facts are stacked pretty high against this guy. They found the man covered in blood not half a block from where Amanda Erickson was found bludgeoned to death. And the murder weapon was found nearby. Like I said, though, Logan hasn't checked him out for motive or any alibis.

"Personally, I think he's good for last night's murder, but we'll have to see about the rest of it. Logan said the man was lethargic and pretty unresponsive when they found him. Leads me to believe that he went on a bender and maybe became psychotic. I understand that can happen with maniacs—psycho one minute and unresponsive the next. Now, my turn. Where exactly are you from?" he asked Blasko.

They talked for half an hour. Blasko and Josephine worked hard to come up with the dullest answers they could to the newsman's questions. Their goal was to make Blasko sound no more interesting than someone's maiden aunt come to visit.

"I don't think anyone can be that boring." Emmett smiled, knowing he was being given the brush off.

"What do you know about Clarence?" Josephine asked, ignoring Emmett's jab.

"So we're back on the murder, huh? Okay, from what I can tell, Clarence is just an ordinary guy. People think he's a little odd, maybe, but that's not a crime and more common than you'd think. But he runs a good garage and, if you ask him nicely and give him a buck, he'll put a little libation in the trunk. The consensus is that he's all right for a guy with a rich jerk for a father."

"Where does he get the booze from?"

"The usual sources. There are half a dozen guys making 'shine within fifty miles of here, and even more that are making bathtub gin. But people respect the fact that Clarence gets it from the more reputable sources. No one's gone blind from what he sells."

"Could there be a connection between Clarence and this guy Floyd Hopkins?" Josephine asked.

Emmett leaned forward. "That's exactly the question I asked Logan. He just waved it off, telling me they were looking into it. I went around and talked to a few of the folks who are regulars at the garage. A couple said Floyd bought booze there. Not that that proves anything."

Blasko had to hold his tongue. He knew that Hopkins had, in all likelihood, been unconscious from loss of blood until he was found. But he didn't know how to get Josephine off of this red herring without admitting what he'd done.

"Maybe Clarence and Hopkins were working together," Josephine suggested.

"I don't know. Clarence comes across pretty clean except for selling some hooch on the side. I can't really see him killing his wife."

"Nothing else about him?"

"Worse thing I could get out of anyone was an old school buddy who said that Clarence had had a strong crush on their teacher."

"What about Carrie?" Josephine asked, switching focus.

"Ahhh, now she's a piece of work. I can't find anyone that likes her. Mean as a water moccasin if you cross her."

"She would seem like a good suspect," Blasko put in. "Upset at her father for something and jealous of Amanda, maybe?"

"Could be. Kind of a Lizzie Borden thing," Emmett mused. "We'll have to see how everything sorts out with Hopkins. Logan isn't one of our greatest minds, but he's dogged. I can't really blame him for focusing on the guy found covered in blood near the murder weapon."

"Any chance Carrie could be in league with Hopkins?" Josephine asked.

"Not likely. Like I said, she doesn't seem capable of getting along with anyone. And she doesn't tolerate fools, and Hopkins qualifies as a fool of the first order. I think if Carrie was planning anything, she'd look for a competent partner."

Blasko was chaffing under the social constraints. What he really wanted to do was to get out of the house and see if he could figure out how Hopkins had been made a patsy by the real killer.

Emmett finally left, assuring them that no matter how boring Blasko might be, the paper was going to carry a small story about him. "Not every town has a baron," he said with a smile, waving his notepad in farewell as he walked down the porch steps.

After he was gone, Josephine turned to Blasko, who tried to find anything to look at other than her eyes.

"What do you think? Did this guy kill Erickson and his daughter-in-law?"

"No," Blasko responded.

"You sound very sure of yourself." Josephine could sense that Blasko was hiding something.

"I am sure that it wasn't Hopkins."

"How can you be so positive?" Josephine tried to get Blasko to meet her gaze without success. "Tell me."

"Not right now," he said, hoping he could find a way to avoid ever telling her.

"I don't like this. If we're playing at being detectives, then shouldn't we share all of our information?"

"Sherlock Holmes doesn't tell Watson everything." Blasko felt ridiculous invoking fictional characters to support his position. *Desperate times require desperate measures*, he assured himself.

"We aren't… Oh, never mind. Do what you want,"

Josephine said, exasperated. She took a few deep breaths to calm herself, then asked, "But if it's not Hopkins, then who?"

"A family member or a known enemy, would be my guess. I need to go out and learn what I can about Amanda's murder," Blasko said.

"There you go again. Off stalking through the night doing who knows what." As she heard herself saying those words, certain pieces seemed to fall into place. "You had something to do with Hopkins, didn't you?" Josephine asked sternly.

Blasko threw up his arms dramatically. It was an old trick that he hoped would work as well in the parlor as it had on the battlefield—when faced with defeat, one should make a dramatic withdrawal.

"What are you accusing me of?" he demanded, confident that she didn't have enough evidence to come up with a good answer.

"I don't know. But you're hiding something."

"Bah! Enough of this talk. I'm going out." Blasko strode from the room, trying to look indignant.

"Fine! Run off. I don't care. I'll conduct my own investigation!" Josephine shouted to his retreating back.

CHAPTER SEVENTEEN

When Josephine turned around, Grace was casually picking up a glass from an end table. "'Bout time you figured out you can't trust that man," she said, wiping off the table where the glass had been.

Josephine just glared at her, causing Grace to huff and leave the room.

Standing at the parlor window, Josephine tried to remember back to when her father was still alive and life had been normal. But it was no use. Now she felt like she had a house full of boarders, each with their own strange agendas. She couldn't imagine when she might ever again feel relaxed and confident of her future.

She slapped her hand against the window glass. *I'll be damned if I'm going to sit around here and just let him do whatever it is he* does, she told herself, turning and stalking off to the kitchen.

"Anna cooked up a ham this morning. Wrap it up for me, please. I'm going to take it over to the Ericksons."

Grace's mouth fell open. Josephine had turned to go before she recovered enough to speak. "Now's not the time for takin' food over there, Miss Josephine. You know that. You're goin' to get yourself in hot water for sure. You know they don't want no one botherin' them tonight."

But Grace was talking to the wall. Josephine was already upstairs.

Half an hour later, she was walking across the street to the Ericksons' house. She'd practically had to wrestle the ham out of Grace's hands. Holding the ten-pound platter and knocking on the door was awkward, but she managed.

Clarence opened the door, looking surprised. "Miss Nicolson, we're…" Then he paused, noticing the ham. The custom of bringing food to a grieving home was well established, so he had no choice but to take it from her. "I'm sorry, but no one is in the mood for company," he said bluntly.

"I just want to give everyone my condolences," Josephine said. When he still hesitated to invite her in, she added, "I'll be quick," and stepped forward, causing him to instinctively back up. She used the opportunity to get past the threshold.

"What do you want?" came a voice from above. Josephine looked up the staircase to the second floor to see a scowling face staring down at her. "Haven't we been through enough?" Carrie asked in a tone that would have caused soldiers to snap to attention as she stomped down the stairs.

"I just brought over a ham for the family," Josephine explained.

"We buried our father today and learned that Amanda was beaten to death. And still you have the nerve to come over here with a ham? You're just a snoop," Carrie said angrily.

Josephine knew Carrie didn't have the warmest personality, but now she seemed to be coming unglued. Josephine knew she was pushing things by coming over this evening, but this still felt like an overreaction.

"I understand—"

"You understand what? You understand what it's like to have two of your closest family members slaughtered in less then a week? I don't think so."

Carrie had pushed forward as she spoke, forcing

Josephine back almost to the door. Josephine looked over at Clarence, but he seemed to be ignoring the whole altercation. Was he used to his sister's outbursts of temper or was he just stunned by the murder of his father and wife? Finally admitting to herself that the visit had been a mistake, Josephine looked for a way to extricate herself before Carrie actually took a punch at her.

"That's enough," Clarence finally said to Carrie. His tone was flat and hard. She wheeled around on him.

"I don't need *your* advice, that's for sure," Carrie said, giving him the same red-hot stare that she'd focused on Josephine.

Clarence didn't back down, returning her fury with a cold look. Josephine thought they might come to blows, but like two wild animals trying to establish dominance without suffering an injury, they both just puffed up and tried to intimidate each other. Clarence blinked first, turning away from Carrie's gaze.

"I think you ought to go," he said to Josephine.

"I'm sorry," she said weakly. But as she turned to the front door, Lucy walked in from the parlor. Her eyes were red, but she gave Josephine a small smile.

"Thank you for being so thoughtful," she said, nodding toward the platter that was still in Clarence's hands. Lucy reached out and gently took it from him.

"We are suffering so much. I don't know what we've done to deserve all of this heartache." Lucy shook her head. "I just have to go on, that's all I can do. Clarence, would you come help me in the kitchen? Carrie, you need to remember, in these trying times we're going to need the goodwill of all of our neighbors."

Carrie looked like she might throw up. She opened her mouth to speak, only to clamp it shut and stalk away.

"I can see that you all want to be alone," Josephine said, opening the door while she tried to separate all of the weird vibrations she was getting from the family.

"Thank you again," Lucy said, while Clarence stepped

over to the door and ushered Josephine the rest of the way out.

Blasko was searching for Matthew, who was now more difficult to find without the strong odor of alcoholic sweat. At last, he discovered him standing on the front porch of an old Greek Revival mansion facing Main Street. A sign out in front of the house read: *Sumter View Boarding House*. There were several old men rocking on the porch and talking. As Blasko approached, he heard words such as "murder," "club," "blood" and "Erickson," but when the men saw him, all the conversation ended.

"You the royal fellow living over at the Nicolson house?" The man who asked had fewer teeth in his mouth than he had fingers on his hands. Grey, scraggly hair fell down from an old, wide-brimmed felt hat.

"I am Baron Dragomir Blasko," he said with a slight bow.

"We don't have no kings and shit on this side of the ocean," a man sitting next to the first man said. He had a huge potbelly, no hat and no hair. His bald pate reflected the light coming through the windows.

"I admire your democracy," Blasko lied. The truth was, he found it all very confusing and, for the most part, a lie. There was clearly still a class system with the black man at the bottom and the rest stratified based on income and family history.

The men laughed and coughed. Matthew stood apart from them, leaning on the porch railing and smoking a cigarette.

"You know anything about these murders?" the potbellied man asked.

"I'm sure I don't know anything more than you," Blasko assured them.

"Hear they got the killer locked up over at the jail. We're waiting to see if there's going to be any action tonight,"

Scraggly Hair said.

"Damn lucky he was killing Ericksons. Not much hot blood in the clan," Potbelly said.

"They killed the mean one. Old Man Erickson might have given the coward a fight for his money."

"You worked for him, didn't you?"

"Hell, yeah, musta been twenty years ago. I did some collection work for him. Someone wouldn't pay, I'd ask Old Man Erickson what he wanted me to do. If there was something to take, we took it. If not… things got broke. That's all I'm sayin'. Now, his daughter, she takes after him."

"I hear that," Potbelly agreed.

They were quiet for a moment and Matthew moved away from the railing. "I think I'll walk down to the jail," he said, stepping on his cigarette butt.

"You'll let us know if there's going to be a lynching?" Potbelly chuckled.

"I'll be sure to tell you," Matthew said sarcastically.

"If you don't mind, I'll walk with you," Blasko said, more for the benefit of the old men on the porch than really asking permission.

"So they caught the killer?" Matthew said, once they were out of earshot of the porch.

"No. They have not."

Matthew stopped walking for a moment and turned, trying to see Blasko's face in the moonlight. "You seem very sure."

"All I will tell you is that the man in jail has an alibi."

Matthew started walking again.

"Are you staying at that boarding house?" Blasko asked.

"Living on the streets doesn't have much appeal when you're sober."

"You have a job?"

"Funny about that. I have a lot of time to fill now. Not drinking is boring as hell. So, yeah, I got a job. I'm working at Kelly's cotton warehouse down on the river. Probably just for a few weeks until they've shipped out most of this year's crop."

"Did you see Thomas Kelly today?"

"No. Wouldn't expect to with the funeral."

Blasko wondered how the funeral had gone. He probably should have asked Josephine. She was supposed to have been there. He tended to forget about events that he couldn't attend, but at eleven o'clock in the morning there was no chance of him being there. He was having a hard time adjusting to living in a world that revolved around daylight.

The courthouse came into sight. Even from several blocks away, they could see bright lights and several people in the town square.

"A lot of unusual activity for this time of night," Matthew observed.

"They wouldn't really hang him now, would they?" Blasko asked.

"Not likely. Logan may not be much good as a detective, but he's not bad when it comes to maintaining law and order. I saw him in action when there was a run on the banks and people were getting a bit twitchy. He deputized a dozen men and had everything on lockdown for over a week. He ran it like a regular military operation. I bet he was hot stuff as a staff officer in the Army."

"Good to know," Blasko said. As they got closer, they could hear yelling.

The sheriff's office and the jail were across the street from the courthouse on the south side of the square. There were a dozen cars and trucks parked out front and several men were standing on the sidewalk, but all the yelling was coming from one man. It was Thomas Kelly.

By the time Blasko and Matthew were crossing the street to join the group, they could tell that the rest of the men were a bit embarrassed by the ruckus Thomas was causing.

"Bring him out here! I'll kill him myself!" Thomas screamed, walking up the steps and pounding on the door of the sheriff's office.

"Thomas, settle down. We're with you, but this ain't helping," said a man wearing an old fedora and brown jacket.

"Logan's going to come out and throw you in jail," warned a short fellow in a dark suit.

"You're all a bunch of cowards," Thomas said, turning and speaking to the small assembly.

"That's not fair," the man in the brown jacket protested. "You know that ain't fair."

Blasko looked around at the gathering of rabble. It was clear from his experience with mobs that only a few of the men seemed close to supporting Thomas. The rest were there for the entertainment.

Before Thomas could turn back to the door, it opened behind him. Sheriff Logan stood inside the doorway, holding a Winchester shotgun.

"Go on home," he said, looking at no one but Thomas, who was clearly surprised to be face to face with the sheriff.

"Give us Hopkins," Thomas said through clenched teeth.

For just one second, Logan's eyes shifted to the group behind Thomas. All of their eyes immediately found somewhere else to look other than at the sheriff. "I think you mean you, Thomas. Nobody else is causing trouble," Logan stated.

"I want him. He killed Amanda Erickson."

"And what's that to you?" Logan asked.

The question took Kelly by surprise. "I…"

"Go home before you embarrass yourself more. You got a wife. I'd suggest you go to her." Logan's voice was dripping with disdain.

Bobby Tucker drove up in his patrol car. Before he could even get out, the crowd had started to move away.

"What's all this?" Bobby said in a commanding voice that caused most of the crowd to quicken their pace as they walked away. Thomas and Logan were still locking eyes on the steps.

"Is that you, Kelly?" Bobby asked as he walked toward the building. Thomas didn't answer him. Bobby turned and saw Blasko still standing off to the side with Matthew. His expression darkened.

Blasko could tell that the deputy wanted to come over and confront him, but the situation with Thomas took precedence. Bobby turned back to the steps and asked the sheriff, "Everything okay?"

"Thomas was just leaving," Logan said. The spell was broken. Thomas turned and bumped shoulders with Bobby as they passed each other.

Blasko and Matthew quickly walked away into the night.

It was midnight when Blasko got back to the house. He saw that the lights were still on in Josephine's room. With a deep sigh, he entered the house and walked upstairs.

"Yes?" Josephine said in answer to his knock on her door.

"It's me." *Why am I always on the wrong side of her door?* he asked himself.

"Just a minute."

Wearing her dressing gown, Josephine opened the door and invited Blasko to sit with her in the window seat. Each related their evening's adventures.

"You need to be careful. The killer is still on the loose," Blasko told her. "Going over to their house was taking a risk."

"The atmosphere over there and the way everyone was acting was creepy as hell," Josephine said, ignoring the warning. As though summoned by the mention of hell, Poe jumped up on her lap, giving Blasko a yellow-eyed stare before nesting in the folds of her gown. "And how exactly do you know that the killer is still loose?"

"I'd rather not tell you," he said

"Are we in this together or not?" Josephine asked, with a slight edge to her voice.

"We are."

"So then why don't you want to tell me?"

He thought of all the honest yet obfuscating answers he could give, but rejected them all. Reluctantly, he said, "I took some of Hopkins's blood last night. I left him in a stupor to the point that he couldn't have killed Amanda Erickson."

Blasko watched Josephine's reaction closely. Her face seemed to vacillate between disgust and anger. "Why would you do that?" she asked, her tone making it clear she'd settled on anger.

"Because the blood that you provide for me is only good enough to keep me alive. Nothing more."

She stood up, displacing Poe. "Let me understand this. You attacked someone and left them helpless because you wanted to feel better?" Disgust seemed to be taking over now.

"I wouldn't phrase it that way," he said, trying not to get angry and defensive. He knew she had a right to feel betrayed.

"I don't care how you would put it! This man is at risk of being hung for a murder he didn't commit because of what you did to him." Josephine was pacing the room in irritation.

"Hopkins is a despicable man." Blasko felt obliged to offer some defense of his actions.

"That's no excuse for you attacking him. He's still a human being, for God's sake."

Blasko narrowed his eyes. "Are you suggesting I am not?"

"I don't know what you are!" Josephine threw out without thinking. Her blood was so hot that she didn't immediately regret the words.

"How dare you!" Blasko stood up. "I have always treated you with respect. I expect the same," he said, his own anger building.

"Respect? You attacked me!"

"Oh, must we always go back to that?!"

"So I'm just supposed to forget that you tried to kill me the first time we met?"

"Bah! I don't have to stand here and listen to your insults

and accusations." Blasko stalked to the door, turning as he opened it. "I would leave here if I could," he said and slammed the door behind him.

"And I wouldn't let you stay if I had a choice!" Josephine shouted after him.

Damn it! Damn it! Blasko berated himself as he hurried downstairs away from her.

CHAPTER EIGHTEEN

Amanda was buried the following Tuesday. Josephine went to the church service and listened as each surviving member of the family came to the pulpit to provide a eulogy.

Clarence told the story of how he and Amanda first met, and talked about how much he would miss her and what she had meant to him. As he spoke, his eyes looked unfocused. To be fair, though, everyone at the funeral seemed dazed by the events of the previous week.

"Amanda had a big heart. I don't think anyone could deny that," Clarence said toward the end of his speech, looking right at the Kellys. They were sitting about halfway back in the church, their bodies rigid in the pew and looking for all the world like people who were waiting for their turn on the rack.

Clarence's expression turned dark as he looked at Thomas Kelly. Josephine wondered how many people in the church recognized the significance of that stare. Probably several. Sumter was a small town and, by now, almost everyone would have heard about the scene Thomas had caused at the jail and guessed the reason why.

Lucy spoke next. She was hesitant at first, but once she got started she told what seemed to be an endless number of stories about her and Amanda. She kept looking over at the coffin as she spoke, which Josephine found a little odd. The casket was closed due to the damage that had been done to Amanda's face. She hadn't suffered quite as much as her father-in-law, but she'd still been struck multiple times. Mr. Connelly had explained to the family that the mortician's art could only do so much.

Last to speak was Carrie, who gave Amanda a much quicker send-off than the others had. She talked about how, though not bonded by blood, they had been as close as real sisters. As she spoke, Carrie looked very uncomfortable, but Josephine wasn't surprised. Carrie seldom attended church and she didn't like talking to people.

Throughout the speeches, Josephine kept glancing at the people around her. If Blasko was right that the sheriff had arrested the wrong man, then the odds were good the killer was in the church. Every time, her eyes kept coming back to the family members.

Could one of them really be the murderer? Did any of them have motives? Of course, the fewer family members there were, the more the family fortune was consolidated, giving an obvious motive for each of them. And, certainly, Clarence as the cuckolded husband had a motive for killing Amanda. For Carrie, the motive could simply be money and her natural hatefulness. What about Lucy? The stepmother who wants all the money? Amanda might have remembered something that pointed to Lucy's guilt in the murder of Mr. Erickson. Josephine could only shake her head in frustration. It was all speculation at this point.

A few of Amanda's friends spoke and the choir sang a couple of hymns. When they were finished, there was a moment of hesitation before everyone decided they could get up and escape the claustrophobic grief that filled the church.

During the service, Josephine had noticed Sheriff Logan and Deputy Bobby Tucker standing at the back of the church with their hats in their hands. As she stood up, she looked again for Bobby. She wanted to corner him and find out about the sheriff's plans regarding Floyd Hopkins. She needed to know if she and Blasko were going to have to find a way to directly intercede on the wrongfully accused man's behalf.

She found the deputy standing outside the church, scanning the parking lot. "Bobby!" He turned when he heard his name.

"Hi, Josie. Is it proper for me to say you look nice today? I never know how to act at a funeral," he admitted somberly.

"Thanks. I think it's always okay to say nice things."

"Where's your friend?" Bobby said, looking around.

In her current mood, she wanted to say that Blasko wasn't her friend. Instead she explained, "He doesn't come out in the sun."

"That's right. Kind of odd." The comment was made as much to himself as to her.

"I think it's safe to say that he has a few quirks."

"I…" Bobby hesitated. "Well, I wanted to ask him if he'd gotten anywhere with his investigation of Erickson's murder."

"You really want his opinion?" Josephine asked, a bit surprised.

Bobby looked down. "I hate to admit this. And please, this is just between you and me, but I don't think Hopkins did it." He shook his head. "Trouble is, the sheriff won't look at any evidence that doesn't point at Hopkins."

"You've gotten evidence Hopkins isn't the murderer?"

"Well, that's just the problem. We got loads of proof that he killed Amanda, but nothing to show that he killed Mr. Erickson. In fact, the man has a pretty good alibi for that day."

"What kind of alibi?"

"Okay, so, he got off work about half an hour before Erickson's body was discovered. It's ten minutes from his job at the feed store to their house. He could have taken five or ten minutes to kill Erickson and then it's just five minutes home. His wife swears she heard his truck pull up to their garage and Hopkins come into the house no more than thirty minutes after he left work."

"So he had the time to kill Erickson?"

"Maybe. But the timeline is tight. And where's the blood? How did he clean up? How can someone kill like that and then be cool as ice when he gets home?"

"I see what you mean. But Sheriff Logan thinks he could have done it?"

"Yeah. He says that the time the body was discovered could have been off a little. And, of course, he says that Hopkins's wife is probably lying for him."

"Sounds possible," Josephine agreed.

"I don't buy it. What's his motive? For Amanda, I might accept the drunken rage argument. But he wasn't drunk when he left the feed store. Everyone agrees that Hopkins drinks too much and is a mean son of a bitch when he drinks. But, and here's the big but, they say he never drinks on the job… ever. Drinks like hell at night and on the weekends, but he's clean and sober during work. So how could he have gone into a drunken rage and killed Erickson in twenty minutes?"

"What does Logan say about that?"

"He dug up some old argument that Erickson and Hopkins had a couple of years ago. Erickson had bought a farm and had a bunch of cows that needed to be fed. Erickson didn't have any intention of keeping them. He just wanted the cows fattened up so they could be sent to the slaughterhouse. He got the feed store to send Hopkins out to feed the cows every day for him. Anyway, at some point, Erickson claimed that Hopkins was skimming off feed and selling it to another farmer. There was a big fight. Erickson wanted the store to fire Hopkins."

"*Was* he stealing the feed?"

"The store says they couldn't prove anything. But at one point, Hopkins told Erickson that if he called him a thief one more time, he'd kill him."

"That does sound ominous."

"Hearing it now it does. But I talked to a couple of Hopkins's co-workers. They said Erickson was over the line and most of them said they'd have punched the guy themselves. Besides, Hopkins isn't the kind of guy that holds a grudge for two years. He might kill you on the spot in the heat of the moment if he was drunk, but he's not going to wait two years and murder you in cold blood."

"Sheriff Logan doesn't see it that way?"

"No. Told me to quit asking so many questions 'cause I was going to give Hopkins's defense ideas."

"Has he charged him? I didn't see that in the paper."

"Not yet. He's waiting on the district attorney to give the go-ahead."

"Logan doesn't strike me as the type to take orders from anyone."

"I think deep down he knows there's something hinky about this."

"I guess I can tell you that Blasko doesn't think Hopkins is guilty either. In fact, he's pretty sure of his innocence," Josephine said, hoping Bobby wouldn't ask her too many questions about *why* Blasko was so sure.

"I wouldn't mind talking to him. If Logan does charge Hopkins, it'll be the devil to pay to get him to change his mind."

Josephine started looking for a way to extricate herself from the conversation. She didn't want to talk about Blasko, and the thought of getting Bobby and Blasko together in the same room made her feel queasy. Most of the mourners were on their way to the graveside service, which gave Josephine her opportunity.

"Are you coming to the cemetery? We'd better get going," she said, and started to walk away.

"Yeah, okay. Can I come by this evening?"

Josephine gave up. She knew he wasn't going to let it go. "Fine. Say eight o'clock?"

Josephine spent most of the afternoon wishing she'd said no to Bobby. Now she was going to have to go down and talk to Blasko, which was the last thing on earth she wanted to do. She'd been avoiding him ever since their last argument. But as the sun settled behind the trees, she got up and stomped down the stairs. She rapped on the door as hard as she could, hoping that she was conveying the proper amount of anger through the door.

"Good evening," Blasko said reservedly as he opened the door.

"I just came to tell you that Deputy Tucker wants to talk to you. He'll be here at eight o'clock," she said as stiffly as she could before turning to go.

"So you're making my appointments for me now?" he said, trying to put a sense of affront into his words. He'd decided that the best defense against Josephine was a strong offense, so he was going to act as offended as possible.

"I guess if you could go out in the sunlight, then you could make your own appointments. However, under the circumstances, that odious duty falls on me," she answered without turning around.

"What does he want to talk about?" Blasko asked, curious in spite of himself.

"Guess you'll find out at eight o'clock," she threw back from down the hall.

Blasko turned and closed the door. *Infuriating woman*, he said to himself. *She really is becoming impossible. So I took a little blood from a horrible person. I should have finished him off and tossed him into the nearest river. That's what I would have done a hundred years ago. I'm getting soft. Which has led me to this.*

He continued to fume as he dressed. *Someone is killing these people and I need to figure out who so I can concentrate on finding a way out of this situation. I can't live under Josephine's thumb forever.*

For a moment, he stood in his parlor and stared at the door, wondering what to do next. He didn't want to go upstairs too soon. If he did, he'd be forced to either talk to

Josephine or ignore her. Neither seemed like an appealing option. Then it came to him—something that would really get under her skin.

He knew she was interested in the case and fascinated with the idea of playing detective. He'd go out and meet Deputy Tucker in front of the house and suggest that they sit on the porch to talk. Josephine would then have to decide if she wanted to come out on the porch, listen at the window or ignore them. Blasko was certain all three options would irritate her.

At seven-thirty, he headed upstairs and walked past the parlor. He could hear Josephine moving around in the room, but ignored her and walked out the front door. Waiting on the porch, he could hear movement inside the house. He smiled to himself, imagining Josephine's dilemma.

At seven-fifty, Bobby pulled into the driveway and got out of his car. That's when Blasko heard someone around the side of the house call out to Bobby, who turned and headed up the driveway toward the back of the house.

"Damn it!" Blasko muttered. He went back into the house, where he found Josephine and Deputy Tucker speaking with each other in the hallway.

"There you are," Josephine said, smiling sweetly at Blasko. "I was taking some trash outside when I saw Deputy Tucker drive up."

"Great timing on your part," Blasko said, trying to keep his voice light.

"I wanted to speak with you about the murders," Bobby said. "What do you know? Josephine says you don't think Hopkins did it."

"Why don't we go into the parlor?" Josephine suggested.

Once they were all seated and a suspicious-looking Grace had brought them coffee, Bobby started over. "With his alibi, Hopkins should be walking free, but Logan just doesn't want to let him go."

"Hopkins didn't kill either of the Ericksons," Blasko said flatly.

"How can you be so sure?" Josephine asked, an innocent expression on her face.

Blasko narrowed his eyes and gave her a look that he meant to convey: *You're playing a dangerous game.*

"I have information from a source that would rather not come forward. Besides, most people would not consider him reliable," Blasko answered.

"Who's that?" Josephine asked, suspecting that Blasko was just making this person up.

"Matthew Hodge," Blasko said, staring levelly at Josephine.

"The town drunk!" she sputtered.

"That's exactly why he would rather not come forward at this time. And, for your information, he's been sober for several days."

"Oh, well, if he's managed to stay sober for a couple of days, that's all right, then," Josephine said sarcastically. She suspected Blasko was just making things up as he went along.

Bobby had been sitting back, watching this odd exchange between Blasko and Josephine. When they finally stopped bickering long enough to stare daggers at each other, he spoke up. "I think there's enough evidence of Hopkins's innocence without Matthew coming forward. The question is, if he didn't do it, then who did? I need to give the sheriff another suspect to get him to let go of Hopkins."

"An external enemy or one of the family. Those are the only real choices. The lone madmen idea seems to have been tossed out with the second victim. Someone is preying on this family," Blasko said.

"I agree. I've identified half a dozen people who had a good reason to hate Mr. Erickson. The problem is, once you kill Erickson, then why kill Amanda?"

"I see your point," Josephine said, forgetting her feud with Blasko for a minute and getting drawn back into the mystery. "If someone hated Mr. Erickson, they might threaten his family or even harm them. But the killer would want Erickson to be alive to see his family hurt."

"Exactly," Bobby agreed.

"So we'd be looking at someone who hated the whole family," Blasko said. "Or, again, someone within the family."

"I thought about that too. But that doesn't make much sense either. If it was Lucy and money was her motive, there still isn't any point in killing Amanda."

"Maybe Amanda knew that Lucy had killed Mr. Erickson," Josephine suggested.

"Then wouldn't Amanda have told Clarence about her suspicions?"

"Okay, then, what about Clarence?"

"He has an alibi," Bobby said. "He was at the garage until right before the body was discovered. Besides, what would be the motive for killing his father? Lucy inherits."

"But he certainly has a motive for killing Amanda," Blasko said.

"The baron's right."

"I assume you're talking about the rumors concerning Amanda and Thomas Kelly," Bobby said dryly. "We know about those."

"Are they just a rumor? Because he—" Before Josephine could go on, Bobby raised his hand and stopped her.

"In my personal opinion, yes, the rumors are true. The two were having an affair. In fact, I think that's where she was headed that morning. From what I've learned, she would leave the house early some mornings, supposedly to go get bread and donuts from the bakery. Interestingly, Thomas Kelly would choose those mornings to leave for work early. He almost admitted as much to us."

"Could one of the Kellys be the murderer?"

"Neither have a motive for killing Mr. Erickson. As for Amanda... I'm no expert, but..." Bobby Tucker paused and looked meaningfully at Josephine. "I believe Thomas was in love with Amanda. Very much in love."

"Which then certainly gives Sarah a reason to kill Amanda," Josephine said, ignoring the look.

"Again, she has no motive for killing Erickson," Blasko said thoughtfully. "But could his murder have given her the idea to get rid of Amanda?"

"Possibly. But when Amanda didn't meet him and he found out she'd been murdered, Thomas went home. He said he was too upset to work. I asked him about Sarah and he said she was absolutely shocked when he told her," Bobby said.

"What about Carrie?" Blasko suggested.

"That's interesting. She doesn't have an alibi for either of the murders... at least not one that would stand up in court. What's missing with Carrie is a motive. If it's the money, then why wouldn't she kill Lucy?"

"Maybe Lucy's in danger," Josephine said.

"Could be. But, so far, Carrie hasn't gotten a dime out of the killings."

"Maybe she's trying to make it look like someone is stalking the family, killing the members randomly. Eventually she'll knock off Lucy and inherit. Of course, she'd still have to kill Clarence."

"Maybe she just likes killing." Bobby looked thoughtful. "Right now, without an alibi, she *is* one of the better suspects."

"What about the illegal booze being sold out of Clarence's garage?" Blasko asked suddenly.

"Is that more information from Matthew?" Bobby asked.

"Not just from Matthew," Blasko said, irritated at their dismissive attitude toward the man. "Which brings up the question of why the sheriff hasn't shut it down."

"We've never seen anything or gotten an eyewitness to come forward. Nor have we gotten any complaints."

"But you know it's going on?"

"We don't know that anything is going on. We know that there are rumors, but rumors aren't evidence," Bobby said unconvincingly.

"Okay, now I'm curious. Why haven't you all staked it out or run a honey trap or whatever it is you call it to catch them?" Josephine asked.

"Josie, you know and I know that people are going to drink. They're going to buy alcohol somewhere. What might or might not be being sold out of that garage is from reliable producers and it's not going to make anyone go blind. It's also right here in town, so folks aren't driving all over the countryside getting into trouble just to have a little fun on the weekend. If we *see* alcohol being sold, we'll stop it. But if we don't see anything illegal, and no one is getting harmed, then we'd be all kinds of stupid to go pushing them out so something worse could come in." Bobby's frustration with the situation was clear.

"Sounds fishy to me. The sheriff getting a kickback?" Josephine asked.

"Don't you dare say that. No, ma'am, he is not. Damn it, Josephine." His face flushed red.

"Just asking," she said innocently.

"To my point, though, could there be someone else who doesn't like the fact that Clarence is running alcohol out of his garage? Maybe a competitor? Or maybe Mr. Erickson found out and threatened to turn Clarence in?" Blasko suggested.

"Two problems with the last one. First, anything going through that garage, Mr. Erickson would have known about. I'd bet you he was getting a cut too. He didn't mind running close to the edge when it came to profitable illegal activity. He got into trouble a couple times trying to cheat folks. Hell, he might have even suggested the idea. And, like I said, Clarence has an alibi."

"Okay, then, what about Blasko's gangster theory," Josephine said. "Clarence is infringing on someone's territory, so they threaten him. He doesn't respond properly and they killed the old man. Still Clarence holds out, so they... What's the term...? Whack his wife."

"Makes some sense. Especially if they want him to keep running the business and just give them a cut. They wouldn't want to hurt or kill him. But could there be enough money to fight over? I can't imagine a small-time hooch operation like that is bringing in enough dough for a gang to want a piece of the action bad enough to start killing people."

"Sometimes, in the mountains of my homeland, there will come a young tough who's just starting out. He wants to make a name for himself and build up his gang. They'll go after another small operation and, when they do, they'll sometimes overplay their hand. They're too violent and overreact to every situation," Blasko said, but even as he expounded on the subject, he didn't think the analogy held up.

"I'll look into the possibility," Bobby said.

"I have another idea," Blasko said suddenly, pausing dramatically. Almost against their will, Bobby and Josephine leaned toward him. "Something else has to happen before the sheriff would consider releasing Hopkins, correct?"

"Yes, and it would need to be soon. Once he charges him, it'd be like pulling teeth to get him to turn the man loose. Logan is a bulldog when it comes to his suspects."

"So why don't I go over to the Ericksons' house and suggest that Hopkins is going to be released and that a new suspect is going to be named shortly?"

"You think it might flush out a bird? But I'm not convinced it's one of the family."

"I agree that there are still other possibilities. So I'd also suggest you go down to the garage tomorrow and pull Clarence aside. Talk to him in a way that others might think he's a prime suspect or, better yet, that he might be naming a suspect."

"Yeah, I can see that. Folks hanging around the garage see me pushing him and next thing you know, the word is all around town."

"And should filter back to any Junior Dillinger hiding in the background," Blasko said.

"That could get Clarence killed."

"And fear might make him talk. Remember, if it *is* gangsters, then he knows exactly what's happening. If he thinks he's in the crosshairs, he might come clean."

"That should shake both branches of the tree pretty good," Josephine said, sounding eager at the prospect.

"This is a dangerous business," Bobby said. "You should stay as far away from all this as possible," he said to Josephine.

"I will not," she responded emphatically. "I'm not some shrinking violet that has be taken care of."

"And if she needs protection, I will be there to provide it," Blasko said magnanimously.

"This is crazy," Bobby said to them both. After a pause, he added, "But I really don't want to see us hang the wrong guy."

"We'll go over there now," Blasko said.

"If they even let us in the door. After my last trip, there's no guarantee," Josephine admitted.

"You've got a point. Drop a hint that you've been talking to me and see who's interested in hearing what you have to say. Not that you wouldn't expect anyone whose family has been targeted like theirs to be interested in the investigation." Bobby thought for a minute. "Probably best if you go over there throwing around the idea there's going to be a new look at everything. Then Clarence will already be nervous when I show up at the garage tomorrow."

"Then we'd better get going," Josephine said, looking at the clock on the mantel. It was almost too late for a social call.

"If you find out anything really interesting, let me know before I head over to the garage in the morning," Bobby said, standing and heading for the hallway. "And don't use the phone. Dolly listens in on as many calls as she can."

"I know all about our operator," Josephine agreed.

"Why would you use something that can be so easily compromised?" Blasko asked as Bobby left through the front door. He had tried using the phone a couple of times and found it an odd and disconcerting way of talking to someone.

"Because sometimes it's easier than walking or driving over to see someone," Josephine said.

"Real communication requires using all your senses, not just your hearing."

Josephine gave him a hard look. "Just because we're working together on this doesn't mean I'm forgetting what you did. We still need to deal with that."

"I agree… Completely," Blasko said with attitude. He wasn't going to let Josephine shame him for something that he needed and that he thought he'd handled in the best way possible.

Josephine picked up on his tone. "I can see we're going to have a lot to talk about when this is over."

"Agreed."

"Okay."

"Good."

"Quit that. It's not funny. Come on. We need to get over to the Ericksons' before they turn in for the night."

Blasko didn't say a word, turning on his heel and opening the door.

"You are one exasperating man," Josephine said, then couldn't resist adding under her breath, "Or whatever you are."

CHAPTER NINETEEN

"Do we have a plan for getting inside the house?" Blasko asked as they walked across the street.

"I'm thinking," Josephine responded, squinting in concentration.

Again, it was Clarence who answered the door. Josephine had been running her brain in high gear, trying to come up with an opening gambit to explain why they were visiting so late.

"Clarence, I am so sorry to bother you again, but Deputy Tucker was over at our place asking all sorts of questions, and I'm absolutely confused by the whole thing. The baron suggested that, since y'all are closer to the investigation with your poor family at the center of it, you might be able to help me understand all the strange questions Deputy Tucker was asking."

Though Clarence had looked like he was prepared to slam the door in Josephine's face, her hurried explanation managed to turn his face from a stone wall into an open door. "I'll be glad to tell you what I can," he said, ushering them inside. "I'm afraid I might not be much help. We thought Hopkins was going to be charged with the murder any day now. No one has told us any different."

Inside, the house was strewn with flower arrangements festooned in black silk.

"I still can't believe what's happened. Dad murdered in this very house and my wife slaughtered on the street. A crazy person has to be behind this," Clarence said, leading them into the parlor where Lucy was standing by the window.

"I'm not sure I can entertain anyone this evening," she said to Clarence.

"Tucker was just over at their house questioning them about the murders," Clarence told her.

"Questioning you?" Lucy exclaimed, putting her hand to her chest. "Why? Did you see something?"

"No, that's just the thing," Josephine said. "We don't really know anything. But from the questions that Bobby was asking, it sounded like they're looking for someone other than Hopkins."

"But they've caught the killer. Surely?" Lucy sank into a large wingback chair.

"I don't think they're so sure anymore," Josephine said.

"But why is he questioning you?" Clarence pressed.

Blasko took the opportunity afforded by Josephine being the focus of their attention to look around the room. In particular, he wondered where Carrie was. He noticed that the door leading into the den was slightly open. Could he see movement in the next room? He breathed as deeply as he could without looking too much like a bloodhound. Yes, he could detect a faint whiff of female scent from the doorway.

Josephine was still talking to Clarence. "Bobby asked me if I'd seen anyone leave your house on the morning Amanda was killed."

"Did you?"

"No. I'd have said something before this if I had. He also asked me if I'd heard anything at your garage the other day."

Clarence leaned forward and looked directly into her eyes. "What do you think he was looking for?"

"I asked him that very question. All he said was that there

are rumors floating around and he needs to check them out."

"But the sheriff is still holding Hopkins, isn't he?" Lucy asked.

"For now," Blasko said, and everyone turned to look at him. "But I don't think he'll be in jail much longer. There was a witness who can give him an alibi."

"For which murder?" Clarence asked.

"I'm not sure. In fact, I'm not even sure where I heard it." Blasko waved his hand. "But the deputy was asking a lot of questions and most of them didn't seem to relate to Mr. Hopkins."

"All of this is just too painful," Lucy said, wiping at her eyes. "It's bad enough that we have suffered two losses in our family, and now the sheriff seems unable to keep that killer locked up. I would find it just too much if he was allowed to walk the streets with us. Samuel always said Logan wasn't very smart. I've got a friend in Montgomery. I swear, if they let that man loose, I'll get the governor himself involved." Lucy sounded close to hysterics.

Clarence went over to her and touched her shoulder. "Lucy, don't worry. This will all get worked out. I'll find the killer myself if I have to. And if it *is* Hopkins... well..." He looked at Josephine and Blasko. "I'll do whatever's necessary to see that we aren't living in the same town as the man who killed my wife and father."

Lucy reached up and patted his hand. Josephine thought that Lucy would probably find another husband without too much trouble. She seemed a paradox—powerful, yet needy.

Blasko also watched the tableau presented by Lucy and Clarence. They seemed close. He thought about Carrie. Did she feel left out? Had she committed the murders as a way to get back at a family that had taken her for granted? And was she listening at the door even now?

Making sure they didn't overstay their welcome, Josephine again apologized for bothering them and she and Blasko made their escape. Once they were out of earshot of the house, Blasko asked, "Is he serious about seeking vengeance against Hopkins?"

"Ha, this is the South. He'd be expected to. Maybe not to kill him, but run him out of town, certainly. In fact, if the consensus around town is that Hopkins did commit the murders, Clarence won't have to lift a finger. The townspeople will do it for him." Caught up in the excitement of the evening, Josephine had forgotten she was supposed to be angry at Blasko.

When they reached her porch, Josephine stopped and turned to face him. She brushed a strand of hair out of her eyes, blown there by a southerly breeze. A cold front would be pushing through during the night, and already there was the sense of an impending storm in the air. Josephine couldn't help but feel that more than one storm was building.

"We're going to have to work this out between us. I can't live like this," she said.

"Let's deal with the murders first."

"Promise me that, until we've talked, you won't attack anyone else."

Blasko winced at the word "attack." "You have my word that I won't seek blood from anyone else until we've finished with this murder investigation," he said, hoping he could keep his word.

"Thank you." She turned and opened the door.

"Wait," Blasko said, cursing himself for what he was going to say next. "I'm sorry if this has hurt you." *Damn her, she makes me weak.*

"It's not just me that you're hurting. Are you coming in?"

"No, I have a few things I want to look into." He saw the look on her face, a fleeting look of suspicion that she tried to hide. "I gave you my word."

She nodded and closed the door.

Blasko headed out through the tree-lined streets. He walked briskly, passing many houses with their lights still on, but he noticed there weren't as many people walking the streets or sitting on their porches as there might have been a week ago.

The murders had been a shock. Sumter was small enough that the majority of the citizens knew Sheriff Logan personally. While they knew that he was a good man, and they trusted him, they weren't so sure he was up to the task of catching the killer. Hopkins had looked like he was good for the murders at first, but the people that knew him, and the people who just liked to stir the pot, had all been saying that the wrong man was in jail and the killer would strike again. The town was balanced on a razor's edge.

Blasko stopped outside the Kellys' house and watched the windows. He could see Sarah Kelly moving from room to room, but there was no sign of Thomas. Blasko was hoping for the opportunity to talk with him. Thomas was a man whose hidden life was now out in the open for everyone to ridicule. He might be in the mood to blurt out everyone else's secrets. Blasko had seen this play out before in the old country. A man caught bedding another man's wife wasted no time telling everyone that the butcher was in love with the maid or the priest was stealing from the parish.

Blasko walked around the house and noticed that a light was on in the garage. Peering in through the cottage door, he saw Thomas sitting on an old sofa, trying to read a paper by the dim overhead light.

Blasko tapped on the door and watched as Thomas almost fell on the floor. His eyes were huge as he stared toward the door, almost as if he feared the killer might be knocking. Blasko rapped again and moved closer to the window so Thomas could see who it was.

"You scared the bejesus out of me," Thomas said, looking puzzled as he opened the door.

"Can I come in?" Blasko asked.

"Yeah, yeah, come on in." Thomas backed away from the door, swinging it wide for Blasko to enter. "You were there the other night, weren't you?"

"The night you were pounding on the jail door? Yes, I

was."

"I guess I was a little out of control." Thomas looked close to tears. "It's just…"

"I understand," Blasko said stiffly, a little worried that he was going to have to console the grieving man.

"I guess everyone knows by now. My wife damn sure does." He indicated the pillows and blankets on the sofa. "I don't know if I'm going to be able to make it right. Hell, I'm not sure I want to."

"You were in love with Amanda?" Blasko prompted. He didn't want to make Thomas more upset, but they needed to get past this part in order for Blasko to get the information he really wanted.

"I knew her from way back when, before she'd gotten involved with the Ericksons. We went to school together. I guess I had a crush on her. Stuff got in the way and I never even asked her out on a proper date. Then I fell in love with Sarah, or at least thought I did, and the next thing I knew, we were married. Then one day I bumped into Amanda and we kinda picked up our friendship where we'd left off. She invited us to start playing cards with them. All innocent at first, I swear. But it didn't take long before we were meeting up to talk, then one thing led to another." He paused and looked up at Blasko. "You don't care about all of this. Why did you come by?"

"I'm still looking for Erickson's killer… and now Amanda's."

"You don't think Hopkins did it?"

"No. Do you?"

"I did. Hopkins is an ass and a violent drunk."

"But you aren't sure anymore if he killed Amanda."

"No. Like I said, at first I could see it. The man is dangerous when he's drunk, but to just attack someone…? I don't know. It doesn't make a lot of sense. I've seen him get into a few fights, and it always starts with an argument, and then he's swinging those big ham hocks on the ends of his arms. He could hurt you real bad with those, but not once have I seen him pick up a weapon. He likes to hit people with his hands. Hopkins wants a fight. I can't see him sneaking up and hitting Old Man Erickson while he was sleeping. That's not Hopkins's style."

"I agree. Which brings us back to who really killed Erickson and Amanda."

"I'd like to know. Whoever it was killed the sweetest woman in the world." His eyes were tearing up again.

"What about Clarence? Could he have killed them?"

"Maybe... I don't know. Clarence isn't that... focused. I don't think he could follow through with it."

"Did he know about you and Amanda?"

"If he did, he didn't care. Amanda said that he didn't have a lot of interest in her. With him, it's all about the garage and whatever he does there. They'd both gotten to the point where they ignored each other most of the time."

"What about your wife?"

"You mean, did she know about Amanda and me? I didn't think so. I thought I was being real sneaky, but now Sarah says she did. Women. Screw me. What she's mad about now is that everyone else knows."

"Could your wife have killed Amanda?" Blasko asked bluntly.

"A week ago I'd have said that she didn't have it in her. But I've learned a lot in a few days." He rolled up his sleeve and showed Blasko a bandage wrapped around his arm. The white cotton was stained with blood. "She went after me with a butcher knife when I got back from the jail the other night. For a minute, I thought she might kill me."

"Can you think of any reason she might have hated Samuel Erickson?"

"No. They were partners sometimes when Lucy and Sam would join us for pinochle."

"Don't you need tables of four? You, Sarah, Clarence, Amanda and the Ericksons make six. Who else joined you?"

"All depends. Usually people who were visiting one of us. It was an irregular thing for the Ericksons to join in."

"But when they did, your wife would be Samuel Erickson's partner?"

"That's usually how it'd work out. We kind of had a rule that couples didn't partner up. Of course, looking back, I'm not sure that was a good idea. Playing together at all wasn't too good of an idea. But Amanda and I would be partners and Clarence usually ended up with Lucy."

"But you just said that couples couldn't be partners. Wouldn't that leave the final couple as partners?"

"That's right, but the rule didn't extend to guests. We learned over the years that strangers to our game were more comfortable if they played together. Guess it all sounds a bit arbitrary now. Maybe it was a rule we made up so that Amanda and I could play together."

"Were there ever any arguments between your wife and Samuel Erickson?"

"No, they were a great team. Usually won. He was tough and was the leader. Sarah is really observant. She'd pick up on every clue he gave her."

"You didn't mind losing to them?"

"We'd switch it around occasionally. Sometimes Amanda and I would be playing Clarence and Lucy or the fourth couple, whoever they were. But no, when we played Erickson and Sarah, it didn't bother me that we usually lost. I just liked sitting across from Amanda." Thomas could no longer keep the tears from streaming down his face. "I miss her so much. I've thought about just starting my car and…" He waved toward the Pontiac that sat only a couple of feet from the back of the couch.

"Why? What would that do?" Blasko was ignorant of the finer points of gas combustion engines.

"The carbon monoxide will kill you in an enclosed space," Thomas said, uncomfortable now that he'd voiced the thought.

"Nonsense. Why would you want to do that? You need to survive," Blasko said. He was not good at comforting people. "You want to live. I'm going to find the killer and, when I do, you'll want to be there to see him dragged off to prison."

"Hung. I want to see him swing from the scaffold," Thomas said with more grit than he had shown since Blasko had arrived.

Blasko stood up and then paused. "What about Carrie?"

Thomas looked thoughtful. "She didn't play cards with us very often. Maybe four or five times in the last couple of years. When she did she was good, calculating. But while she was a good card player, she was a poor partner. She was rotten at coordination and communication. Also, you could tell that she hated to lose. Once, she got so mad at me that she quit and went to her room."

"Did she and Amanda get along?"

"I thought so. In a way, she got along better with Amanda than her own brother. Not that Amanda and Carrie had anything in common. Amanda was personable and sensitive while Carrie is cold and determined. When I say she's cold, I don't mean like my wife is being now. It's not personal. Carrie just doesn't seem to like people very much. Or maybe she just doesn't need people. Amanda did."

"Could you see Carrie committing the murders?"

"Funny, but I can't say. On the one hand, I think she could do something like that in a… detached way. But on the other hand, she'd have to have a good reason for doing it. She lacks… passion."

"Thank you," Blasko said and stood to leave. Then he looked at the Pontiac. "What you should learn from these terrible events is that life is precious. Hold on to it. Make use of the gift."

Back at the house, Blasko went to the closet in his room and opened a small wooden box. He took out the small bone button he'd found in Samuel Erickson's bedroom. There were still a few cream-colored threads in the four holes.

Blasko held the button up to his nose and smelled it, sensing a feminine perfume. Had he smelled it before? While his sense of smell was formidable, his memory sometimes failed him. He looked at the button again. Why had it been lying beside the bed? Had it fallen there or been placed there? Either way, it could point to the killer.

CHAPTER TWENTY

For Josephine, the next couple of days felt like being inside of a boiler with the pressure building. Many of the townsfolk were waiting for Sheriff Logan to officially charge Hopkins so that they could breathe easier and move on to the trial. In the South, trials—even ones where the crimes were particularly horrible—were seen as a form of entertainment that could keep everyone busy with news and gossip for a month.

But in this case the consensus wasn't complete. A lot of people just didn't believe Hopkins could have committed both crimes. And, if that was the case and the wrong man was in jail, then there was still a killer walking the streets. A murderer who could sneak into your bedroom in broad daylight and club you to death in your bed, or creep up behind you on the street and crush your skull. Anxiety and fear ruled the day.

While the nervous town seethed, Josephine tried to keep an eye on the Erickson family. But it wasn't easy since they had pretty much locked themselves inside their house.

On the second night, Bobby Tucker came to her house.

"Logan's going to charge Hopkins with the killings. He was meeting with the district attorney all afternoon about it."

"For both murders? What evidence do they have against him for Mr. Erickson?" Josephine asked, appalled that the man could be tried on no evidence she could see.

"The iron pipe. If we link the murder weapon from the second murder to the first, then we've got a clear line between the two."

"And the pipe was used in both killings?" Blasko asked.

"Yep, according to Dr. McGuire. He sent the pictures up to Montgomery to have a state pathologist look at them. He confirmed that both sets of wounds could have been made with the same weapon. And we found blood matching both victims inside the pipe.

"But the DA told Logan they should just go with Amanda Erickson's murder because Hopkins doesn't have any semblance of an alibi for that one. He's afraid that if they link the two cases, and the jury doesn't believe Hopkins could have committed the first murder, then they'll let him off on both charges."

They heard the phone ring in the kitchen. Josephine didn't immediately get up to answer it, hoping that Grace would get it. She had been working with the maid to get her to answer the phone. However, Grace didn't like it, so the experiment hadn't been going well. This time, Josephine was lucky and the phone stopped on the fourth ring. A minute later, Grace came running into the room.

"A man on the telephone says there's an emergency for Mr. Tucker. Wants to talk to you right now!"

Bobby followed her into the hall. Blasko and Josephine could hear his side of the conversation from the parlor.

"What now? Who? What're they driving? On my way."

Bobby turned away from the phone and almost ran straight into Josephine and Blasko, their faces lit with curiosity.

"What's happened?" Josephine asked.

"We just got a call that Carrie has taken Lucy hostage and is headed out of town," he answered breathlessly and without stopping.

As the door slammed behind him, Blasko and Josephine looked at each other for a split second before Josephine ran through the kitchen to the back door where the key to the Chevrolet was hanging. Blasko was right behind her.

"Do you want me to drive?" he asked.

"Are you out of your mind?" was Josephine's shouted answer.

Blasko opened the wooden doors of the garage as Josephine got into the car and started the engine. "Hurry!"

Blasko jumped into the car as it rolled down the driveway.

"Come on, close the door. He's already heading down the street."

They could see Bobby's taillights as his car headed south out of town. As soon as Josephine had the car out of the driveway, she put her foot down on the accelerator. The car jumped and lurched, but as soon as she caught the gears up, they went roaring down the road behind him.

They caught up to the deputy within minutes. His old patrol car was no match for the big Chevrolet and its powerful engine. They kept pace with him for several miles until Bobby's taillights suddenly seemed to grow huge in the windshield.

"He's stopped!" Blasko yelled, terrified.

"No, he's just turning," Josephine said, slamming on the brakes as she fought with the steering wheel into the turn. "He's heading toward Cotton Dock."

The drive seemed to take forever. Josephine's knuckles were white as she held the steering wheel in a death grip, hunched over and peering through the dim light cast by the headlamps.

Blasko kept a firm hold on the dashboard as they bumped along.

"Don't brace yourself like that. If we get into a wreck, it would just break your arms."

"So my choices are to smash against the dashboard or have my arms snapped in two?"

"Pretty much!" Josephine shouted over the noise of the car.

Blasko saw the juke joint rush by. Several folks stood out by the road, watching the cars roar past them in the darkness.

Bobby's car started to slow down. Josephine followed him into the parking lot of Kelly's cotton warehouse. Two other cars were already there, parked at odd angles. By the time Josephine stopped her car, the deputy was already out of his and another car was pulling into the lot behind them.

Bobby had his revolver drawn and was looking toward the warehouse, but he turned back when he heard Josephine open her door.

"What the hell are you doing here? Get back in your car!" he hissed at her.

"You heard him," came the gruff voice of Sheriff Logan as he and Deputy Paige stepped out of the car behind them.

The sound of a gunshot came from the warehouse. The sheriff and his deputies rushed forward, Logan drawing his Colt 1911 as they stalked toward the building. Josephine and Blasko ignored the order to stay in their car and got out, standing beside it.

The moon provided some light, but there were plenty of dark shadows where a person could easily hide. That was where Blasko's superior night vision gave him an advantage over the others. He squinted, but didn't see anyone in the shadows or lurking under the loading dock that wrapped around the building.

He moved forward as the three lawmen climbed cautiously up the ramp. Sounds of scuffling could be heard from the other side of the building. The men picked up their pace, letting their handguns lead them.

"Help!" someone shouted. The word worked like a throttle, launching the lawmen into action.

Blasko tried to stay close behind them, hearing more gunshots. As he rounded the corner of the building, he saw the sheriff and his deputies with their guns drawn and Carrie clutching her chest. She dropped the shotgun she'd been holding, and only then did Blasko notice that Lucy was lying at her feet. As Carrie sank to the ground, she gurgled once and then fell prone onto the deck.

For a moment, everyone stood silent, staring at the bodies sprawled on the loading dock in the moonlight. Slowly, Lucy began to struggle and moan, breaking the spell and causing the lawmen to move forward.

Sheriff Logan knelt beside Carrie. "She's dead."

Lucy's hands were tied and her mouth was stuffed with a gag. When Bobby pulled the cloth away, she gasped for air before shouting, "Clarence! Where's Clarence? She shot him!"

The deputies swapped glances with the sheriff. None of them had seen Clarence.

From his spot by the warehouse wall, Blasko looked over the side of the wooden platform. Clarence was lying on the ground five feet below. Blasko jumped down, drawing everyone else's attention.

"He's alive," Blasko reported. "It looks like he's been shot in the head."

Clarence groaned in response. "The shotgun went off, but I think it just grazed me. Lucy, are you all right?" he called.

"Yes! Thank God you're okay," Lucy said.

"I must have passed out. How's my sister?"

"Sorry, son, but she's dead," Logan said, looking down at Clarence and Blasko.

Bobby jumped down and helped Blasko to lift Clarence and carry him back to the cars where they could get a better look at his injuries. They laid him down on the ground and turned on all the car headlights. Above his right ear, his scalp was bloody and singed.

"She just went crazy," Clarence explained. "Over the last day or so, she'd been acting peculiar. Then tonight she grabbed Dad's double barrel and tied me up. She said she hated me. Then she grabbed Lucy and ran off. I don't understand any of this."

Lucy was kneeling beside Clarence. "Clarence managed to get loose and chased us out here, trying to stop her."

Clarence was rocking back and forth on the ground. He touched his hand to his head and moaned.

"Don't worry yourself. We'll get Dr. McGuire to look at you," Logan said.

"I got close enough to grab the shotgun. Carrie was fighting me for it and it just went off."

"You're lucky to be alive."

"Poor Carrie. I don't know what happened to her," Lucy said. "She's always been odd, but why would she do this?"

"I think it's safe to assume that she also killed her father and Amanda too." Logan looked at Deputy Paige. "Willard, go back to town and get Dr. McGuire. Also, have Emmett Wolfe from the paper come out here and take pictures for us. But don't let Wolfe do anything but get his camera. We don't need the whole damn town out here."

Clarence struggled to stand. "I'll help in any way I can," he said.

"Just wait for Dr. McGuire to get here. I want him to take a good look at you."

"I think I'm fine. Got a hell of a headache, but that's the worst."

Logan looked at Lucy. "Would you like Willard to drop you off at your house?"

"If Clarence is all right with me leaving?" she said, more to Clarence than to Logan.

"I think it's safe now," Clarence told her, giving her a small smile.

Deputy Paige and Lucy left in Logan's car. Bobby and Logan turned their focus to Josephine and Blasko.

"You shouldn't have followed me," Bobby scolded her.

"Sorry."

"I don't know what you were thinking, young lady," Logan barked.

The group settled into an awkward silence. They were all

relieved when Dr. McGuire finally arrived, followed closely by Deputy Paige with Emmett Wolfe in tow.

"What are you two doing here?" Emmett asked Blasko and Josephine when he walked up.

"Don't worry about that right now. I need you to stop being a reporter and be a photographer," Logan ordered

"Sorry, Sheriff, I don't work for you."

"You do now. Raise your right hand," Logan said.

"Are you kidding?" Emmett said, astonished.

"I don't have time to get anyone else out here right now. I'm going to swear you in while you take the pictures. After that, you can go back to being a newsman."

"I don't know."

"I'll give you the rights to some of the pictures. Ones I pick," Logan bargained.

"Deal."

They had to break into the warehouse to turn on the dock lights for the photographs. Blasko and Josephine watched for a while, then Blasko approached Bobby.

"Come and see me when you're done here."

Bobby was surprised by the request, but it had already been such an odd night that he just nodded.

CHAPTER TWENTY-ONE

Josephine and Blasko rode back to town in silence for a while before she said, "Seems strange."

"I know." Blasko watched the road.

"Not that Carrie doesn't seem plausible. But there's something not quite right about all of it."

"At least Hopkins will be released."

"Yes, that's good news. And now you won't have to fess up and try to explain why he couldn't have done it," Josephine said dryly.

"I don't know how we're going to resolve this."

Josephine wasn't sure if he meant the murders or their domestic issues. She decided to go with the one that she most wanted to hash out at the moment.

"You could stop attacking people. That would be a start."

"I told you, I'm not sure I can," Blasko said, his voice tired. "I tried the blood you got for me. It works… but only up to a point."

"I'm sorry. I can't see how you can change my mind on this."

"Hopkins is not a nice person."

"There are a lot of men who aren't nice."

"Precisely."

"But you can't go around assaulting people just because they aren't nice!" Josephine's voice was rising along with her blood pressure.

"But I need to."

"How long do you think you can get away with biting people on the neck and leaving them lying around?"

"You're being hysterical," Blasko said, afraid that her anger would start to affect her driving.

"Don't you start."

"If I learned to drive, then I could take blood from people farther away," he said, believing he was offering a reasonable solution.

"I don't think you understand where I'm coming from. I don't want you attacking anyone… period."

"Then you shouldn't use the argument that I'll get caught as a reason not to do it."

"I'm just trying to point out to you that there are multiple reasons not to do it. One of many is that I won't stand for it. Why do you think I'm getting you those blood shipments?"

"Because you don't have a choice."

"I have a choice."

"Now you are just being blind. We've gone over this."

"And you promised me you would be fine with the blood I got for you."

"I said that the blood would keep me alive. I never said I would be fine. Besides, I didn't know. I've never tried to live exclusively off of dead blood before now. I'm weak. My senses are not what they could be." His accent was deepening with his frustration. "I do not know what you want of me. I have explained to you what I am and what I need, yet you feel compelled to revisit this question."

"We're revisiting it because you changed the rules."

"Do you want me to lie to you and tell you that I will not do it again?"

A part of Josephine *did* want that. It would be a simple, short-term solution. But the stronger part of her wanted to hash this out, to have it settled once and for all so she could move on. Finding out about Blasko's attack on Hopkins had shaken her trust in him. *But why did I trust him in the first place?*

She hadn't told him, but she'd ordered a rare book from a New York bookseller entitled *The Lore and Legend of the Carpathian Mountains*. She wanted to find out for herself if everything Blasko had been telling her was true.

"I don't know what I want," she finally said. "How's that for honesty?"

"It's a lie. You want me to change," he said, his tone aggrieved

"Fine! You're right, I want you to stop doing dangerous things that could get someone seriously hurt or killed and that just might land you and me in mortal danger. I can't even imagine what would happen to us if someone discovers I brought a blood-sucking monster back from another country."

"How dare you?" His eyes flashed. "You would also have to tell them that you have my blood running through your veins."

"At least I don't go around killing people." Josephine felt lost in this endless argument.

"I haven't killed anyone! Recently… And I would not be troubling you if you hadn't bitten me."

"Enough! I agree with you. There, how's that? I agree with you. Do you know what I agree with? I agree that this is a stupid topic and we should stop bringing it up," Josephine said with finality.

At last, Josephine pulled the car into her driveway and back into the garage. It was almost one in the morning and everything was quiet. The night owls had gone to bed and the early risers, those who made the bread and delivered the papers, hadn't yet started their day.

Exhausted by their unwinnable argument, Josephine and Blasko entered the house in silence and went their separate ways.

Two hours later, there was a knock on the exterior door to Blasko's basement apartment.

"You wanted me to come by?" Bobby Tucker said.

"Come in."

Bobby entered the room, giving it a thorough visual examination.

Blasko retrieved a small box and opened it, taking out the button he'd picked up in Samuel Erickson's room.

"What's this?" Bobby said, looking back and forth from the button to Blasko.

"I found it in Mr. Erickson's bedroom when I went up and looked at the body. It was lying near the nightstand."

"And you just took it?" Bobby exclaimed, his face turning red.

"You all had already been in the room and were off chasing your hobos," Blasko said dismissively.

"You had no right!" Bobby said, not letting go of his anger.

"I'm giving it to you now. You might not have it at all if I hadn't kept it," Blasko said coldly.

"So why are you giving it to me now?"

"I think you will find that it came off of a garment belonging to Carrie."

"That's what you think, is it?"

"I doubt you'll have a hard time finding the clothing."

Bobby stood there, studying Blasko's face. "What makes you so sure?"

"I'd rather not say."

"You know I'm not a dummy." Bobby's anger was rising again.

"Perhaps. Your sheriff, however…"

Bobby took the button and put it in his pocket. "We're searching Carrie's rooms now."

"Where are Mrs. Erickson and Clarence?"

"She's at the house. Dr. McGuire took Clarence over to his office to dress his wound."

"Carrie's body?"

"That went with McGuire to his office. He'll do a full autopsy tomorrow."

"And what does the sheriff think?"

"We have witnesses who saw Carrie driving the car through town. One of them even saw Lucy in the passenger seat. Clarence followed them. It seems pretty cut and dried. Especially if you're right about this button. Carrie didn't have a good alibi for either of the first two murders, and I think the sheriff is going to be satisfied with how the case is coming together."

Bobby noticed the smirk on Blasko's face. "What? You see something different?"

"Proving my theories is the difficulty. Did you search Clarence before you let him go to Dr. McGuire's office?"

"Nooooo. Not that he could have been hiding too much. McGuire flushed the wound at the warehouse, so Clarence had to pretty much strip down except for his pants. Why? If you think you know something, you need to tell me now."

"I don't *know* anything. I suspect a lot."

"I suspect some things myself," Bobby told him, his eyes cold. "And what the hell is that squeaking sound?"

Blasko ignored the annoyed deputy. "You can suspect what you want," he shot back.

"If you get Josephine into trouble, then I'm going to make you pay. Is that understood?"

"Ahhhh. Now you are speaking your mind. The relationship that exists between Josephine and myself is none of your business."

"I'll tell you what is my business and what isn't," Bobby said, his anger boiling. "I don't know what your deal is, but I don't trust you. And I'm not the only one around here who thinks you're more than a little odd."

"I've had some experience with villages like this. You all might do well to look beyond your own dirt roads. I'm here for as long as I want to be here. But I am no threat to you or to anyone else that doesn't interfere with me."

"Josephine means something to me and to a lot of other

folks here in town. Let me be clear, we're keeping an eye on you."

"Bah! Keep an eye on me. I'm going to solve these murders and it's up to you if you help or hinder."

This gave Bobby pause. He wanted to arrest the right person for the murders, and he'd been disappointed with the sheriff's performance so far.

"I'm not going to cut my nose off to spite my face. If you know something or find out something about these murders, then come to me. I'll listen to you. I'll give you that much." His words were clipped and professional.

"When I know who the murderer is and have proof, I won't keep it from you." Blasko was growing tired of Bobby.

Apparently, the feeling was mutual. The deputy gave Blasko one last look before turning and walking out. Over his shoulder, he muttered, "Get that damn squeaking fixed."

As the door closed, Blasko whistled and Vasile flew down from the rafters and landed on his arm.

"Did you have good hunting tonight?" Blasko asked. The bat squeaked in response and settled down to clean his face and wings.

Blasko sat down in a chair, his back rigid and his eyes open. He replayed the night's events in his mind, picturing the scene at the warehouse as a series of still images. He listened again to the words that had been spoken.

Abruptly, he stood up and looked at the clock. It was almost four in the morning. Time—he couldn't give the killer time. But the sun would be up in just a couple of hours.

"Go now. I have more to do tonight," he said, encouraging Vasile to find a new perch.

Blasko hurried out of the basement and up the stairs.

"What? Stop that!" Josephine yelled, grabbing a dressing gown and throwing open her bedroom door in response to Blasko's pounding.

"Come now. We have to get back out to the warehouse," Blasko said, his accent strong in his urgency.

"What's going on?" Grace called down from the third floor, her voice edged with fear.

"It's nothing, Grace!" Josephine shouted up to her.

"Tell me that man isn't wakin' us God-fearin' folk up at this hour for some more craziness." Her voice had changed from fear to irritation.

"Go back to bed!" Josephine yelled. "Can't it wait?" she said in a loud whisper to Blasko.

"No. I think I know where there is evidence that can prove who the killer is. But we need to hurry or it could be gone."

"Give me five minutes."

Blasko went back downstairs to wait for her. The clock chimed four, causing him to run back down to his room to grab a handful of the native earth from his coffin. "Just in case," he muttered to himself as he put the dirt in his pocket.

CHAPTER TWENTY-TWO

Ten minutes later, Josephine and Blasko were rumbling out of town once again in the Chevrolet.

"I *will* learn to drive," he told her over the roar of the motor. Josephine just nodded, keeping her eyes focused on the two beams of light piercing the darkness in front of the car.

There weren't any other cars when they got to the warehouse, but a thick rope had been strung across the entrance to the parking lot with a crude, hand-painted wooden sign hanging from it that read: *Closed by Order of the Sheriff.*

Blasko leapt from the car and removed the rope.

"What are we looking for?" Josephine asked him after she parked the car. She was carrying a railroad lantern that gave off a yellow light that barely pushed back the darkness. She was grateful for the little bit of heat it gave off. She hadn't had time to throw on anything more than slacks, a shirt and a light coat.

"Back by the dock. Where the shooting took place," Blasko said, walking quickly while his eyes scanned the dark. The light from the lantern was actually making it more difficult for him to see.

"I didn't ask where, I asked what," Josephine said, trying to keep up.

"I'll tell you when I find it," he responded cryptically.

"This better not be a wild goose chase."

Once they were near the spot where Clarence had been lying, Blasko got down on his hands and knees and started moving over the ground. At one point, he crawled under the loading dock.

"Here!" he yelled triumphantly. Crawling back out, he held a Smith & Wesson Army revolver wrapped in a handkerchief. "Clarence buried this a couple of inches down in the dirt."

"He had a gun?"

"Yes, I had a gun," said a voice from the darkness behind them. "And I have another one now. So, please, drop that one."

Not having much choice, Blasko dropped the gun.

"Clarence?"

"Yes, Josephine. You and this freak just had to stick your noses into everything. Now it's going to cost you your life." Clarence stepped into the moonlight. His head was bandaged and he held a Colt 1903 automatic in his hand.

"Don't be an idiot," Blasko said, putting himself between Clarence and Josephine.

"Shut up and get back."

"Everyone knows what you've done."

"Nonsense. You might have made some good guesses, but that's all you've got." Clarence sounded sure of himself.

"Of course, you aren't the one who came up with the plan, are you?" Blasko said, causing Clarence to twitch. For a moment, Josephine thought he was going to shoot Blasko right then and there.

"I told you to keep your mouth shut, you damn foreigner." Clarence was practically growling.

"You're nothing but a spoiled rich boy," Blasko said, moving forward and trying to keep Clarence's eyes locked on his. Blasko knew he wasn't close enough yet to get the jump on Clarence. He wasn't worried about himself, but Clarence could still manage to get a shot off at Josephine. Blasko wouldn't take a chance with Josephine's life.

"Stop it!" Clarence said, not making it clear if he meant Blasko's words or his approach.

"She came up with the plan, didn't she?"

"I'm not going to warn you again."

She? Josephine thought, then some odd images began to surface from her memory. She thought she might be sick.

"It was you and Lucy," Josephine breathed, her voice barely conveying all of the shock and disgust she felt.

"Both of you, walk toward the river," Clarence said, stepping to the right so that he had a clear shot at both of them.

Blasko moved, willing to go along with Clarence and wait for his chance. He had to keep Clarence's attention focused on him.

"Lucy killed Samuel, didn't she? Did the two of you always plan on killing Amanda and Carrie?"

"Amanda had to go. Carrie could have waited, but we needed a scapegoat after Hopkins fell through."

"I'd ask why, but I assume that you and your stepmother are… unnaturally close. I heard you had a crush on your teacher in school. Have you always had a thing for older women?"

"Damn it! I told you to be quiet. Less talking and more walking," Clarence ordered.

Blasko had hoped that Clarence would be tempted to strike him. If he came closer, it would be the opportunity Blasko needed.

"How did you figure it out?" Josephine asked Blasko. She was having a hard time finding her way in the near dark. The moon was setting, and there were a lot of shadows cast by the pecan trees that filled the small area between the warehouse and the bluff overlooking the river.

"I've had my suspicions for a while. The button I found was too convenient, which belies his story that Carrie wasn't marked from the beginning."

"It was always a backup plan," Clarence grumbled.

"However, my proof came tonight. After the shooting, when Clarence was being treated for the damage done by the shotgun to the side of his head, he was speaking with everyone normally."

"And…"

"If a shotgun had been fired that close to his face unexpectedly, he would have probably lost most of his hearing, at least temporarily."

"You're right," Josephine said, irritated at herself that she hadn't noticed it.

"I realized that the shotgun blast to the side of his face was just a ruse. Clearly he'd had time to pick up some of the cotton and put it in his ears before the gun went off."

"Perfect. It wasn't like there aren't tufts of cotton lying all over the ground," Josephine said.

"I'm surprised Lucy would let you do that," Blasko said, turning to face Clarence. They were halfway to the river bluff.

"I told her I wasn't going to lose my hearing over this. Now move!" he said, and stopped until Blasko started walking again.

"So now you're going to the gallows," Josephine said.

"No, I'm not. You two are going in the river."

Blasko nodded. "I see. You plan on getting us in the river somehow and then pushing our car in after us. Not the worst plan. Not that you have much choice at this point."

"Keep talking. I don't mind putting a bullet in you right now, 'cause with the currents, nobody is going to find your body before it has rotted to bones."

"You paint a grim future for us."

"You're in love with your stepmother, which is just sick, so you all decide to kill your father, your wife *and* your sister?" Josephine said, unable to hide her revulsion.

"Was it Lucy's idea to have you on the ground so that you could shoot Carrie when the sheriff showed up?" Blasko asked.

"That was my idea."

"You had to make sure she was dead," Josephine said, her mind rapidly filling in the plot. "You two kidnapped *her*. Lucy had the gun in the car and put a gag around her own mouth. When they were driving through town, it looked like she was the victim, when in reality she was holding a gun on Carrie down low so that no one could see it."

Blasko picked up the narrative. "Then when the sheriff and his deputies arrived, they gave Carrie the empty shotgun while Clarence held the revolver on her from down below, out of sight of the deputies. When Clarence pulled the trigger, Logan and the deputies also fired. Everyone was shooting at virtually the same time. It was almost foolproof. If Clarence had fired and the lawmen hadn't followed suit, Clarence could have just said he'd grabbed the revolver when he went in pursuit of Carrie after she kidnapped Lucy."

"You think you're so damn smart," Clarence snarled.

They were almost to the bluff. Blasko looked down the twenty feet of sandy slope to the water below. He turned back to see Clarence raising the gun toward them.

"I'm sorry," Blasko said to Josephine, reaching over and pushing her gently down the bluff.

As Josephine rolled down toward the water, Blasko leaped at Clarence, who managed to fire two rounds before being tackled. One bullet pierced Blasko's chest while the second ripped through his left shoulder.

Ignoring the red-hot pain coursing through him, Blasko slammed his head against Clarence's forehead while trying take the gun away. Their wrestling match seemed to go on forever, until Blasko elbowed Clarence in the nose. There was an audible snap and Clarence released his hold on the gun. Blasko grabbed it and stood over him.

"Fawkan brawke ma nos," Clarence mumbled, rolling around on the ground in agony. Blasko gave him a swift kick to the ribs for good measure.

"Are you all right?" said a worried voice from behind him.

Blasko turned to see a sandy and disheveled Josephine, breathing hard.

"For me, these are just flesh wounds," Blasko said, reaching for her hand. The pain from his wounds was excruciating. He looked toward the east. Even now, a faint blue tinge of color was evident on the horizon. "I don't have much time. We need to tie him up. Hold this."

Blasko handed her the gun and grabbed Clarence's leg with his good arm. Josephine followed as Blasko dragged him toward the warehouse. Clarence whined until Blasko threatened to kick him again.

At the warehouse, they found some rope and used it to tie and gag Clarence. He looked at them in defiance, but couldn't fight them both.

With Clarence finally secure, Josephine turned her attention to Blasko. "Let me see your wounds," she said gently.

Blasko took off his coat and pulled his shirt open to reveal the oozing holes.

"You'll heal?" Josephine asked, concern in her voice.

"With fresh blood." Blasko looked meaningfully at Clarence. "If I take enough from him, he won't remember anything from the past hour. When I feed, it releases a small amount of toxin that causes a mild form of amnesia. That's why Hopkins didn't remember what happened."

"So there's a two-fold advantage to you taking Clarence's blood," Josephine said, looking down at the man. His eyes were wide as he looked back and forth between them, trying to scream around his gag.

"Yes. But I'll do whatever you say," Blasko said sincerely.

"There's no real choice. You're just making it so that I have to tell you it's okay," Josephine said. After a moment, she gave a small nod.

"You know I have to," Blasko said as he knelt beside the squirming Clarence. Josephine turned away, cursing herself for being a hypocrite who could condone the behavior but wasn't willing to witness it.

Forcing Clarence's head to the side and exposing his neck, Blasko bit into him and drank, feeling the life force flow into him. His wounds would take a day or two to fully heal, but he was already feeling relief from the pain. He forced himself to stop drinking just before he crossed the line that would have ended Clarence's life.

"I can't stay here and there's no time to get back to the house. I need to go someplace where I'll be safe for the day," Blasko said, standing to face Josephine as he wiped the blood from his lips. He could already feel the heat of the rising sun, even though it was still a quarter of an hour before it would crest the tree line.

"Where?" Against her will, Josephine was already feeling a sense of dread at being separated from him.

"Not far," Blasko said, acknowledging their blood bond. "But away from here. They might search the grounds."

"What do I tell them?" Josephine asked, looking down at Clarence's unconscious body.

"Tell them what happened, only without me in the story," he said with a small smile, then trotted off into the woods.

Josephine took a deep breath and walked up to the warehouse. She managed to undo the jury-rigged lock from the sheriff's earlier break-in, then slipped in to use the phone. Once she got ahold of Bobby Tucker, she told him her location and that she'd been attacked by Clarence. Josephine hung up before Bobby could ask too many questions.

A mile away, Blasko found an old wooden shack raised just off the ground on pilings. He crawled underneath and dug as much of a hole as he could. Spreading the dirt he'd brought from his coffin into the hole, he crawled in after it and lay face down. Soon he fell into the light trance that engulfed him every day as the sun took over from the night.

No one really believed Josephine's story, but they couldn't get her to change it. And the fact that she was giving them the killers went a long way toward quelling their suspicions. By midday, Dr. McGuire had managed to revive a still weak Clarence, who was too groggy to deny the murders and implicated Lucy within an hour.

That afternoon in the sheriff's office, Sheriff Logan and Bobby Tucker grilled Josephine one more time.

"I'm still trying to understand this. You overpowered Clarence and got his gun away from him? Is that what you want me to believe?" Bobby asked her.

"Bobby, you saw how he was. I don't think he was in his right mind when he found me." Josephine tried to sound as honest as possible. "I don't know if he'd been drinking or what."

"Why the hell did you go back out to the warehouse?"

Sheriff Logan was sitting on the edge of his desk, watching Josephine. He hadn't gotten anywhere with the woman himself, so he'd asked Deputy Tucker to take over the questioning. He knew they had a history and thought that maybe Bobby could use their relationship to get her to tell the truth. For his part, Logan hated questioning women. He wasn't even sure when his own wife was telling the truth, let alone a strange woman. And as far as he was concerned, Josephine Nicolson was one of the strangest.

"I thought that I saw a flash from below the loading dock when y'all shot Carrie. So I decided to go back and investigate."

At the mention of Carrie, she saw both men cringe. They now knew that Carrie was innocent, which meant that her death was at their hands. Neither of the men liked to think they had shot a defenseless woman.

"Did your friend Baron Blasko go with you?"

"No. I told him what I'd seen and he agreed that it was odd. As you know, he already had his own suspicions about the whole thing. But he told me to wait and go back today for a look around."

"Then why didn't you do that?"

"I just couldn't go to sleep thinking about it. I thought if I went out there and looked around, then I could get it out of my head and finally get some sleep."

"Then Clarence showed up and pointed a gun at you?" the sheriff interjected.

"That's right. He started babbling about the murders. He seemed delirious."

The sheriff and deputy exchanged looks. Clarence had certainly been half out of his mind when they found him. He hadn't been able to tell them anything about that night. Dr. McGuire had put it down to a concussion received from the shotgun blast. Luckily, the two small marks on Clarence's throat were chalked up to powder burns.

"This whole thing is screwy as hell," Logan said. "And that blasted baron's 'suspicions!' Tell me again how he knew that Lucy had gone to the bathroom after attacking her husband."

"He didn't know it was Lucy. He just knew that *someone* had, and he figured it was probably someone who felt comfortable in the house."

"You said he saw that the sink was wet?" Bobby said.

"That's right." Josephine certainly wasn't going to tell them that Blasko could smell the blood trail from the bedroom to the washroom.

"And Blasko suspected Clarence and Lucy of working together?" Bobby asked, still very uncomfortable with the relationship between Clarence and his stepmother.

"Not a first. But when he realized that Clarence could hear after having the shotgun fired off so close to his head, everything fell into place. Because if Clarence was lying about what happened that night, then Lucy had to be in on it too. I admit, when I realized he was right, I could remember a few times when Lucy and Clarence had acted a bit strange together."

"And exactly when did Blasko tell you all of this?"

"Like I told you, Sheriff, he followed me out to the warehouse. He heard me when I left the house and realized where I was going."

"But he showed up *after* you'd clobbered Clarence." Logan's eyes were just slim slits of suspicion at this point.

"That's right. By the time he was able to get a ride out there, it was all over. But that's when he told me his theories."

"Who drove him out there?" Bobby asked.

"Thomas Kelly," Josephine said without hesitation. She had called Kelly after she hung up with Bobby. After she had explained everything, he was more than willing help them out by saying that he'd driven Blasko down to Cotton Dock. By that point, Josephine had been pretty sure the gossipy operator would have been too busy connecting calls for the sheriff's office to listen in.

"So with the killer tied up, the baron just decided to go about his business and leave you to handle the aftermath?" Bobby said in disbelief. "Where the hell is he now, anyway?"

"He had an emergency out of town, but he'll be back soon. I'm sure he'll be able to answer all of your questions once he returns." One thing Josephine was sure of was that Blasko would be able to come up with enough half truths and possible truths to satisfy them. After all, they had their killers.

"Humph!" Logan muttered. He wasn't entirely happy with the situation, but he didn't feel like he could pressure Josephine any further. Besides, things were wrapping up in a pretty convenient, if somewhat odd, package that would make his office look good in the eyes of the townsfolk. The office of sheriff was an elected position, so he always had to keep his eye on the prize.

Logan looked over at Bobby, who gazed back with a *What the hell can we do?* expression on his face. "Show Miss Josephine out," Logan finally said. But looking at Josephine, he added, "That will be all for now, but make sure that the baron comes in here as soon as he gets back, or I swear to the almighty I'll put a warrant out for his arrest."

Bobby turned to Josephine once they were out in the hall.

"I don't know what sort of hold Blasko has over you, but always know that, if you ever need help, I'm here."

"I'm fine," Josephine said. "I appreciate your concern, Bobby, really."

"You should know that other people have voiced some concerns about the baron."

"Whatever you've heard, you can forget it. I'm fine and the baron is… fine." Josephine wondered who'd been talking. Her nosey neighbor Evangeline? Could Grace have gone to Bobby? Maybe. Maybe it was both of them. But then she had to admit that Blasko didn't exactly hold himself back. It was possible he'd pushed any number of people too far.

"You bitch!"

Bobby and Josephine looked down the hall to see Deputy Willard Paige dragging a struggling Lucy to a cell. She'd spotted Josephine and wasn't going to miss the chance to tell her what she thought of her investigative skills.

"You and that foreign freak will burn in hell! Clarence loves me and we'll kill you all if we get the chance." After every other word, she slapped at Paige.

"To hell with this," Bobby said, reaching back and slugging Lucy hard enough to cause her head to snap. She rubbed her jaw sullenly, finally allowing Deputy Paige to drag her down the hall to a cell.

Bobby looked back at Josephine. "Clarence is still chained to a bed at Doc McGuire's. We're hoping his memory might improve as he recovers."

That would be very awkward, Josephine thought, hoping that Blasko was right about how much Clarence would forget.

EPILOGUE

Josephine faced a harsher critic at home. Grace met her at the door with squinted eyes and pursed lips.

"I hope we've seen the last of him."

Josephine was exhausted, but she knew she had to deal with this now. "Blasko solved this murder. He's helped us and the whole town without taking any credit. You've made it very clear how you feel about him, but I'm telling you right now, I want you to give him the benefit of the doubt."

"I don't know if..." Grace shook her head.

Josephine didn't have the energy to argue with her. "He's coming back, so you need to wrap you head around that. I appreciate the fact that you've kept your word. I know we can work everything out, but you have to meet Blasko halfway."

"Now Miss Josephine, you know I've only ever looked out for you. You've been kind to me, and I thank you for that. I just wish... I don't know that I can stay here if he's comin' back. I just don't."

Josephine was well aware of Grace's moods and she knew she was being sincere about her fears.

"I know he's different. Maybe even... worrisome. However, he's here to stay. I can't ask him to leave and, after what he's done, I don't want to. So you'll have to decide what you need to do."

Josephine turned and went upstairs, leaving Grace standing at the foot of the stairs.

Blasko returned home two nights later. His clothes were filthy.

"How are you?" Josephine asked. She had hurried down to his room as soon as she heard him enter the house. For the past two days, she'd felt an emptiness inside her that was relieved only by his return.

He took off his coat and opened his shirt. "I'm healing."

The bullet wounds were red and swollen, but closed over. Josephine's eyes widened as she noticed all of the other scars on his body. In places there seemed to be scars on top of scars. She reached out and touched an old jagged line across his abdomen.

"A Turkish kilij. The man was very brave, but had no clue what he was up against. When his sword slashed me, I grabbed it and pulled him off balance. He stumbled and I rammed a dagger into his back. Sadly, I had to toss his body off of the parapet down amongst his men in order to convince them that the battle was over."

"Do you remember them all?" Josephine asked softly, tracing another old wound with her finger.

"No. I remember the brave men and the strong women, but not the rest."

He reached out and took her hand. His eyes held a strange fire as he looked at her. "Josie, we cannot let ourselves be at odds. Good can come from our union, but only destruction from our strife."

Josephine didn't resist as he lowered his lips to her own. Her mind may have been conflicted, but not her heart.

Baron Blasko and Josephine return in:

KNIVES
The Baron Blasko Mysteries–Book 2

Cover design by Corvid Design
Cover illustration ©2019 Duncan Eagleson

ABOUT THE AUTHOR

A. E. Howe lives and writes on a farm in the wilds of north Florida with his wife, horses and more cats than he can count. He received a degree in English Education from the University of Georgia and is a produced screenwriter and playwright. His first published book was *Broken State*. The Larry Macklin Mysteries is his first series and he released a new series, the Baron Blasko Mysteries, in summer 2018. The first book in the Macklin series, *November's Past*, was awarded two silver medals in the 2017 President's Book Awards, presented by the Florida Authors & Publishers Association; the ninth book, *July's Trials*, was awarded two silver medals in 2018. A member of the Mystery Writers of America, Howe is also the co-host of the "Guns of Hollywood" podcast, part of the Firearms Radio Network. When not writing or podcasting, Howe enjoys riding, competitive shooting and working on the farm.

CPSIA information can be obtained
at www.ICGtesting.com
Printed in the USA
LVHW110844180120
644101LV00002B/459

9 780999 796849